Praise for the Author

"Goss's greatest strengths, which are significant and not easily mastered, are authentic dialogue and solid plotting." —BlueInk Review

"Her [Goss] manner of developing her plots and her characters is sure, polished, and yet with enough co-existing suspense to hold our attention to the last page."—San Francisco Review of Books

"This author [Goss] does a fantastic job at creating realistic characters…"—Portsmouth Review

"Goss is a talent; she knows not only how to grab your attention but how to keep it."—Red Headed Book Lover

"Fatal Limit is a fast, captivating and thrilling read and a mystery that young and old will really enjoy."—Readers' Favorite Reviewer

Fatal Limit

Inge-Lise Goss

Olivebranch Press

DEDICATION

To my daughter, Nicole.

ACKNOWLEDGMENTS

As always, my gratitude goes out to my outstanding editors, Jeff LaFerney and Nancy Buford. Their suggestions, comments, and edits greatly enhanced my story. I also want to extend a special thanks to Kelly Pedersen for generously answering my medical questions. Last, but not least, I'd like to thank Margaret Daly for designing an awesome cover.

Chapter 1

The late September drizzle turned into a downpour. Umbrellas knocked into each other as their owners pushed through the crowd to get into the best position to cross the street first when the light changed. A few teetered on the curb, ready to spring at a moment's notice. Horns erupted in the rush-hour traffic. The drivers had no intention of slowing down despite the weather. A woman slipped on the wet sidewalk and grabbed the arm of the closest passerby to prevent her from falling on the hard cement. The stranger gave her an indignant sneer, pushed her hand away, and hurried to the bus shelter to get out of the rain. In the process, he bumped into me as I sat on the dry bench, watching the mayhem unfold. Without giving even a hint of an apology, he bent his head toward me. His steely gray eyes bore into me as if the whole incident was my fault.

Ignoring him, but determined not to move closer

to the edge of the bench to give him enough space to sit down, I gazed across the street, searching for Sheila, my best friend's aunt, to emerge from the hospital. Her shift should have ended thirty minutes ago. I'd intended to wait in my car, but couldn't find a parking spot with a view of the hospital's employee entrance, so I'd parked in the lot behind the bus stop, walked to the bench to avoid the rain, and watched for her.

More people poured into the bus shelter, blocking my view. I stood and peered between the heads of two women just as a bus cut to the curb. No longer able to see the other side of the street, I moved away from the horde of people, opened my umbrella, and headed toward the crosswalk.

I saw Sheila emerge from the hospital and waved my hand in the air. With the rain and people scurrying about, I doubted she could see me in the crowd. Continuing along the sidewalk, I kept my eyes on Sheila and noticed she wasn't wearing a raincoat or making any attempt to cover her head. That seemed odd. Her dripping wet hair clung to the top of her nurse's uniform, and she was staggering, her body swaying with each step she took. Keeping her in my sights, I made my way to the crosswalk. Sheila stopped walking and looked back toward the hospital. A few seconds later, she swung around and moved in a zigzag path to the street. Sheila didn't stop when she reached the curb.

Standing on my side of the street, I screamed. "Stop!…Stop, Sheila!"

A woman next to her gripped Sheila's arm and said something to her.

Sheila violently pushed the woman away, sending

the helpful stranger into the crowd behind her.

Horns blared. Brakes squealed. Tires screeched. But it wasn't enough to prevent a black sedan from smashing into Sheila. Her body flew in the air, landed on the car hood, and slid to the pavement.

Screams of witnesses pierced the night.

The second the light changed, I rushed across the street and pushed my way through the crowd that had gathered around Sheila. Her motionless body lay sprawled out on the wet asphalt. Water-saturated blonde hair covered her eyes and nose. A trickle of blood ran from the corner of her mouth. Before I reached her, a voice bellowed over the crowd behind me.

"Move. Get out of the way. We need to get through."

Two men dressed in green scrubs pushed a gurney toward Sheila. Silently praying she wasn't dead, I backed away and worried about my best friend, Maddie. Even though Sheila was only eight years older than Maddie, she had become her niece's guardian after her brother and his wife were tragically killed by a shooter attacking patrons attending a concert. Sheila loved Maddie as if she were her own child and helped her become a nurse. Sheila even played a role in getting Maddie a job at Feister Northwest Hospital.

I tried to get a glimpse of the green-scrub-clad men checking Sheila, but the noise and mayhem created by the people swarming around made it a difficult task. I backed away from the crowd.

Waiting for the paramedics to assess Sheila's condition, I thought about her. A tall, stunning blue-eyed blonde attracted many men, but boyfriends seldom lasted more than a few months. She had an elitist demeanor and treated Maddie and me like we were still kids, which annoyed me. But when Maddie had called and asked if I would pick Sheila up and take her out for a few drinks since Sheila was having a bad day, I'd agreed.

A policeman directed the crowd to back up as the gurney moved through it. Sheila lay stretched out on it with tubes attached to one of her arms. An oxygen mask covered her nose and mouth. Seeing she was still alive, I felt a sudden weight lifted from my shoulders and followed the gurney.

I stayed behind scrub-clad men as they raced through the lobby. The emergency double doors opened and the gurney was pushed in. A nurse stopped me before I could enter. "Are you related to Sheila Wilson?"

"No. I'm a friend of the family." Sheila was in no condition to give anyone her name, but I figured the staff must have known her.

The nurse directed me to a waiting area in the lobby.

Knowing that it was against hospital policy to give out the condition of a patient to anyone except relatives, I took a seat, pulled out my cell phone, and placed the dreaded call. After a high-pitched voice answered, I said, "This is Dora Stephens. I'm a friend of Madilyn Wilson. May I please speak to her? It's an emergency regarding her aunt."

"Maddie got a call from a nurse on duty in the emergency room. We're all praying for Sheila."

"I'm in the hospital lobby, and I'd still like to talk to her. Is she there?"

"No. She left right after she got the news. She's

gone to the surgical waiting area on the fifth floor. "

"Thanks." Assuming Sheila had been rushed into surgery since Maddie wasn't with her, I disconnected and called Maddie's cell phone. It went straight to voicemail, so I left a message, letting her know I was on my way to the fifth floor waiting area. As I slipped my raincoat back on, Maddie emerged from the elevator.

Fearing the worst, I hurried toward her. Tears streamed down her face. I wrapped my arms around her. "Oh, Maddie, I'm so sorry I couldn't get to her sooner."

"She walked..." Maddie snuffled "...right out in the street. Last night...last night...she was so happy. Something happened...after she got here...that made her upset...but she'd never kill herself." She held a handful of tissues and dabbed one over her eyes.

Wondering what had happened, I led her to a couch, and we both sat down. She leaned on my shoulder and sobbed into my raincoat. In the investigation business, I had often tried to comfort clients when they received bad news about a loved one. But with Maddie, I couldn't think of anything to say to help ease the pain.

As she continued crying, I ran the terrible event over in my mind. Sheila always had a confident feminine walk, like a model. When she staggered toward the oncoming cars, I knew something was off. Why would Sheila wander out into the street? A woman had attempted to stop her. Sheila had knocked away the woman's hand. Was she after something on the other side of the street? Or was she completely disoriented? Drugged? Then Maddie's boyfriend sprang into my head. "Does Tobias know?"

"No. Can…can you call him?"

Caressing her arm, I pulled out my phone and delivered the bad news.

"I'm on my way." The connection went dead.

A middle-aged woman in a nurse's uniform came toward us. She carried a raincoat and a purse. The woman looked at me. "Maddie left in such a hurry that she forgot her things." After placing them on the couch, she gently stroked Maddie's hair. "Sweetie, I'm so sorry for your loss."

Maddie slightly nodded her head as the tears continued to flow.

About fifteen minutes later, Tobias entered the hospital and glanced around. The second he spotted us, he rushed to Maddie and lifted her out of the seat as he wrapped her in his arms. "Sweetheart."

"What am I…" she began, and through her sniffling, I couldn't hear anything else she said to him.

Keeping her close to him, he turned toward me. "I'm taking her home."

I rose and helped Tobias slip the raincoat on Maddie. As I put the strap of her purse over her arm, she gazed at me through puffy eyes. With trembling lips, she said, "Dora, find out what happened."

"I will." I knew Maddie would want me involved. We often talked about some of my investigations. She was almost more excited than I was when my name appeared in a newspaper article, giving me credit for locating a kidnapped two-year-old toddler. She clipped the article, highlighted my name, and stuck it on her fridge. Even though Mason Grover, my boss and president of Grover Investigations, didn't like any of his investigators to be mentioned in any publication, I still thought it was cool seeing my name in the paper. He wanted his investigators to keep a low profile and never draw public attention. I preferred to work in the shadows. Sometimes it was easier to get certain types of information if no one suspected I was a private investigator.

Before agreeing to do any investigation, my first step should have been to clear it with Grover, but in this case, that seemed like a moot point since I had no intention of not proceeding if he didn't give me the okay. I'd be doing it on my time anyway. Still, I decided to call him in the morning to let him know about it. Not wanting to step on any police detectives' toes, I needed to tread carefully until I knew what the coroner listed as cause of death.

Since I was in the hospital and so was Sheila's body, I figured I'd do a little snooping around before calling it a day. My first investigation had involved a malpractice suit. As I was nosing around in a hospital lab—a place non-employees weren't allowed—I was caught by a pathologist. In order to prevent that from occurring again, I needed a uniform. I glanced at my watch—8:32 p.m. Guessing the medical supply store down the street was still open, I stood and left the hospital. Seeing the rain had stopped, I walked at a brisk pace along the sidewalk. To my relief, the store was open. The sign near the entrance noted that it closed weekdays at 9:00 p.m. I only had ten minutes to make my purchase, but I knew exactly what I needed.

On the way back to the hospital, I detoured to my car and tucked my purse under the front seat. Then I headed across the street to the employee entrance and discovered it was locked. A scan-lock was attached the wall next to the door. Irritated by my miscalculation, I lingered close by until a man showed up and swiped his badge over the scan-lock. Right before the door slammed shut behind him I stuck my foot in and pushed it open. My eyes drifted around as I strolled down the hallway, searching for a women's restroom. What I found was better—a women's locker room. I hurried in, placed the store bag on a bench, and changed into my newly purchased blue scrubs and a pair of flat shoes.

As I put my clothing in an empty locker, a middle-aged, heavyset nurse walked in. Blood stains were splattered all over her uniform. To prevent her from seeing my face, I immediately turned toward the locker and began straightening the clothing inside.

The nurse went to another aisle, and then I heard the sound of metal clanging together and assumed she was getting into a locker. Figuring a badge would be needed in order for me to move freely about in the hospital, I quietly waited to see if she planned on showering.

Bare feet padded on the tile floor, followed by a squeaking noise, and then came the sound of splashing water. I went to the last locker in my row and peeked around it. Scattered clothing covered the second bench. I stealthily edged toward it, snatched her badge from her uniform, and crept back to my claimed locker. Since she had seen me by that locker, I grabbed my clothing and moved it to another locker, farther away from her.

Ten minutes later, I stood outside the double doors leading to the hospital morgue, perked up my ears, and listened intensively. Not hearing any voices, I slowly opened a door and saw a small area with file cabinets on one side and a bench on the other. At the end of it was another set of double doors. One was slightly ajar. As I carefully stepped through the first doorway, a muffled male voice drifted out the other set of doors. While I inched closer, the voice became louder. "...you should have..." was followed by sniffling sounds.

Not wanting to eavesdrop on some poor man who was mourning the passing of a loved one, I backed away.

"Sheila...Sheila...I never should have told you," the voice said, stopping me in my tracks.

As I crept closer to the door again, he went on. "Why, oh why, didn't you listen to my warning?"

I bumped into a garbage can, tipping it over. A thud reverberated through the room. A second later, the interior double doors flew open.

Chapter 2

Out through the double doors strode a tall, distinguished-looking, dark-haired man, graying at the temples. His piercing, brown eyes bore into me. He walked with authority, pushed the hallway doors open, and left, appearing too angry to bother with me.

He must've had a thing going with Sheila. What had he warned her about? A person? Could he have prevented her death? Or did he play a role in it? More questions about the distinguished-looking man kept bouncing into my head. Had anything suspicious been discovered by the police in the early stages of their investigation?

I stepped into the morgue. A covered body was stretched out on a stainless steel table closest to me. The other tables were empty. If more corpses were in the hospital morgue, they were being kept cool in a refrigeration unit against the side wall. Doubting the body in front of me would be left unattended very long, I cringed and raised the sheet. With the exception of a bruise on her chin, Sheila's face appeared as beautiful as ever, not how I had expected her to look after being hit by a car, thrown into the air, and smashing down on the pavement.

In case Sheila's death was ruled as nothing more than an accident and a toxicology test wasn't ordered, I decided to retrieve a tube of Sheila's blood. I had learned the procedure one summer when I'd worked in a nursing home. I glanced around the room for what I needed to handle that task and then headed to the sink. Hanging by it was a container that held latex gloves. I pulled out a pair, tugged them on, and found everything else in a cabinet next to it.

Within minutes, I had the blood sample. Slipping the tube into my pocket, I heard a door creaking open. I dropped the syringe into a red sharps disposal container, the latex gloves in a garbage can, and stood next to Sheila's body.

Wearing a white labcoat, an elderly man with a stern expression on his face strolled in. "What are you doing in here?" Anger in his voice put me on edge.

"A dear friend of mine is Sheila Wilson's niece. She's having a hard time accepting that her aunt is dead and asked me to verify the identity." I turned toward the body. "She is still very lovely, isn't she?"

"You are not allowed in here," he huffed. "Get out before I call security."

I exited the first set of doors without saying another word. With the test tube secure in my pocket, I didn't want to take a chance of being stopped by a security guard. I picked up my pace. Hurrying out the double doors to the hallway, I bumped right into a uniformed policeman. "Excuse me." Edging around him, I pressed my lips together when I saw Stan Lindgren, a police detective who had recently transferred to the local precinct. I had met the bold, stocky man at a retirement party.

He tilted his head and furrowed his brow, but he didn't say anything. Hoping that meant he hadn't recognized me and not wanting to give him the opportunity to study my face any longer, I bent my head and walked away from him although I had the urge to run.

While waiting for the elevator, I doubted that I had needed to collect a sample of Sheila's blood since it appeared the case had been turned over to a detective, a good sign that Sheila's death was being looked at as more than an accident. The officers on the scene must've discovered something suspicious that required a detective to be brought in.

Still mulling it over, I rode the elevator to the first floor and headed toward the women's locker room. I slowed down when I saw the owner of the badge attached to my uniform, swinging her arms, gesturing in the direction of the locker room, and chatting with another nurse.

"How dare he suggest that I was careless and left it someplace!" Her frustration was clear in her tone.

From past experience, I knew not to abruptly change direction because to do so would draw unwanted attention. I straightened my collar, making sure that my forearm covered the badge, proceeded to the locker room, and gave the two nurses a pleasant smile as I went by them.

* * *

Recognizing several cars parked along the street in front of my place, I figured a poker game was in full swing inside. Before climbing out of my car, I thought about what, if anything, I should tell Tucker, my live-in boyfriend. He was a police detective and worked at the same precinct as Stan Lindgren. Sometimes Tucker would jokingly say that I let him move in just so I had an inside track on police investigations. Tucker seldom shared information with me that wasn't public unless I was working on the same investigation for a client and I had something to offer him. Then we exchanged information. Some clients hired Grover Investigations before the police had finished doing their job. They claimed the police were working at a slow pace, and they were tired of waiting for their cases to move forward. I was well aware that the police department had been underfunded for years, and their workload continued to grow but not the workforce. As a result, cases took longer, people became frustrated, and Grover Investigations thrived.

Climbing out of the car, I decided not to say anything to Tucker about Sheila or my new case since they never got along.

The minute I entered the house, Tucker greeted me as he dealt another hand, "Hey, Dee. Early ladies' night out? Sheila's fault?"

Unless he was on official police business, Tucker was known for not talking in whole sentences.

"Yeah...yeah," I stuttered, and then drew in a deep breath. "I guess you could say that. Winning lots of money, Tee?"

When I first met Tucker he couldn't remember my name, but he recalled it started with a "D." Instead of asking for my name again, he went the macho way and called me Dee. So I began calling him Tee. Those nicknames had stuck between us.

Tucker smiled at his three buddies sitting at the table. "Not yet."

"Well, then, I better leave you to it." I went to the kitchen, put the test tube in a plastic container, and hid it in the vegetable drawer at the bottom of the fridge. Then I headed to the den and started a file for my new client, Maddie. Even though Sheila often irked me, she had taken Maddie under her wing and treated her like a daughter. I wanted to cry with Maddie. All my instincts told me that something was wrong the minute I'd laid eyes on Sheila leaving the hospital. There was never a question that an investigation was in store for me when I heard she had died. Keeping my wits about me meant keeping my emotions under control, which was essential if I hoped to solve the case. There would be time for mourning and tears later.

After scribbling some notes, I called Tobias to see how Maddie was doing.

"Not well. I gave her a sedative. Now she's sleeping." Tobias was a medical student, and I knew Maddie would be well taken care of in his hands.

"I went to the hospital morgue and ran into a man who appeared to be mourning Sheila's passing. Do you by any chance know the name of Sheila's current boyfriend?"

"Aaah. Jared Ebert. A married man."

A high-pitched wail punctuated the last sentence. I thought it strange until I realized it was Maddie's cat. Probably begging for food. Tobias excused himself and I waited impatiently as the snapping sound of a can being opened came through the airwaves.

Finally, he came back on the phone. "Now where was I. Yeah, Jared Ebert. Romeo is a cardiac surgeon. Sheila was on his surgical team. According to Maddie, Sheila wasn't the first nurse he'd messed around with. He gave her the usual lines that cheating guys often do—she was his true love...he was going to divorce his wife...blah blah blah."

"She actually fell for that?"

"Yes. She had planned to go with him to a medical conference next week. Some problem about that trip arose this morning that made Sheila very upset. Maddie thought that maybe Jared had broken up with her. That wasn't it. Sheila was close-mouthed about it but did tell Maddie that Jared would fix it."

I had always believed that I was the main person Maddie confided in. I felt pangs of jealousy that Tobias knew more than I did. On the other hand, it was good that she shared so much with him because he cared deeply for her. He had asked her to marry him a few times, but Maddie didn't want to talk about it until he finished medical school. She thought if they got married before then, it might cause him extra stress—not *being* married, but *getting* married. Tobias came from a large extended family. His parents had often hinted that they would be happy to pay for everything if their oldest child, Tobias, and Maddie decided to get married. From what Maddie had told me, Tobias's parents were anxious to become grandparents.

"I want to make sure that Jared Ebert is the guy I saw in the morgue. Can you describe him?"

"I've never met him, but Maddie pointed out Romeo once in the hospital parking lot when he was heading to his white Porsche in the reserved section for doctors. He's in his early forties, tall with brown hair that looks like it's starting to turn gray. Maddie says he has a dignified bearing. That probably happens when you make plenty of bucks and marry a woman from a wealthy family," he snorted.

I detected a little resentment in his voice. "What do you know about his wife?"

"Only what Maddie's told me. Her maiden name is Colleen Feister."

My eyes popped wide open. "Is she related to Raymond Feister?"

"Daughter." He paused. "Maddie's stirring. I want to check on her. Hope you can find out what went down this evening."

"That's the plan. Thanks for the info. Give Maddie a hug from me."

"Will do." He disconnected.

I leaned back in the desk chair and thought about Jared Ebert, the star surgeon at Feister Northwest Hospital, founded by his wife's grandfather. Colleen's father, a well-known, influential man in the city, was chairman of the board and also a doctor. Tobias implied that Colleen was partly responsible for all of Ebert's wealth. Had he married her when he was in medical school? Or before he'd even started?

Sitting up straight, I clicked on my computer. Since he was a renowned cardiac surgeon, it didn't take long to locate his picture and bio. Jared Ebert definitely was the guy I had seen leaving the hospital morgue. His bio went on at length about his professional life. Outside that, it mentioned he was married, but not his wife's name or if they had any children. But from it, I learned the year he was born and the year he graduated from medical school.

Doing the math, he was twenty-six years old when he graduated. I grabbed my notepad and began making a list of things I needed to research about Jared Ebert, starting with the year he married Colleen Feister. Jealousy was often a strong motivation for murder. Did Colleen have any medical training? Something Tobias had said bounced into my mind—Sheila wasn't Jared's first affair. How many more had there been and who were the women?

As questions continued popping into my head, I kept jotting them down. Before I finished, Tucker opened the door. "Thought you went to bed."

"Poker night over?"

"No. Need another beer. Go to bed." He sauntered closer and gave me his seductive, mischievous smile that I loved. Tucker caressed my arm. "Fun time comes early tomorrow."

"You have to work on Saturday?"

"'Fraid so." He bent down, raised my chin, and kissed me. "Need to get back."

"I'll be going to bed soon." I cocked my head and smiled at him. "Don't worry. I'll be well rested by early tomorrow morning."

"Counting on it."

I stared at his back side as he left the den. Even though Tucker hadn't played football since high school, he still had a firm, muscular body and the physique of a running back. If anyone who had committed a crime tried to run from Tucker, it would be no contest. Tucker would overtake his perp. Besides being a fast runner, his tackling ability was impressive and often resulted in an injured assailant.

Thinking about what Tucker said, his "early" was around five a.m., so I stuck my notepad in a folder and, with a smile on my face, headed to bed.

Chapter 3

The next morning, feeling completely sated, like I'd finished an energetic workout, I basked in Tucker's embrace.

He kissed my forehead. "Sorry, Dee, I need to get going."

I had the urge to beg him to stay home for a few more hours, but I figured his workload wouldn't allow that. "Any chance the department might hire more detectives?"

"We *did* get Stan Lindgren. You met him at Randy's retirement party."

"He took the place of your colleague who just retired. The number of detectives never increased." My stomach churned, fearing Lindgren would mention something to Tucker about Sheila's death and, if Lindgren remembered seeing me at that party, he would probably also say he saw me at the hospital. Then I'd have a lot of explaining to do. Tucker hated being blindsided and finding out about my investigations from a colleague. Lindgren had been introduced to quite a few people that evening, so even if he did recall seeing me there, he might not remember my name. I decided to take my chances and not enlighten Tucker about Sheila since the police were investigating her death and I didn't want him telling me to stay out of it. Like Tucker, I didn't share anything about my cases with him unless I wanted information. Some of the cases handled by Grover's investigators were of a personal nature—cheating wives or husbands—while others were initiated to determine if a crime had been committed such as a partner embezzling or an employee stealing trade secrets. There were also those that involved a theft where the client wanted the item recouped without bringing in the police.

After Tucker kissed me goodbye, I climbed out of bed, showered, dressed, and headed into the den. The first thing I wanted to do was track down the year Jared married Colleen Feister. I went to the county records and searched for Ebert's marriage license. I struck gold with only a couple of clicks probably because Ebert and Feister weren't common last names. They were married the year Jared turned twenty and Colleen twenty-one. Interesting. He married young. Heck, they both married young. According to Jared's bio, he would have still been in college that year. He hadn't started medical school yet. Did he go after Colleen because she was from a well-off family? Or did they fall in love and just couldn't wait to get married?

Next, I did a Google search for Colleen Feister Ebert. Numerous sites appeared. Most were about social events she had attended with her father or husband. Clicking to the various sites, I couldn't find any pictures of Colleen with Jared. There were a few where she accompanied her father. Based on the date of the events, I knew those pictures were taken before she married Jared. Colleen was a cute teenager with long, brown hair. Then I clicked to her Facebook page. No profile picture. Her bio stated that she was a registered nurse, and it also showed the name of her alma mater and the place where she worked—Feister Northwest Hospital. Did she really work there or did she mention that just to beef up her profile? Unless I became one of her friends on Facebook, I couldn't see any more information about her on that site. I tapped on her Twitter link. She used the same bio there, also no picture. I scanned down to check items she posted and ran across a picture of two well-dressed couples seated at a table covered with a white linen tablecloth and a small flower vase in the middle that held a single rose. They were raising champagne glasses in a toast motion. I immediately recognized Jared. The restaurant had a sleek, upscale interior. The place didn't look familiar to me. The caption above the picture read "Celebrating Georgina's new job at Feister Northwest Hospital."

The two women sat across from each other. They appeared well-dressed and sophisticated. As my eyes focused on them, I could tell the one with the shorter hair, warm smile, and rosy cheeks was an older version of the teenager in the picture with her father. Colleen wasn't as gorgeous as Sheila but definitely attractive. Since the group was seated, I couldn't get a sense of her physique. The other woman with the shoulder-length hair had a round face with puffy cheeks, and I thought she might be on the heavy side. Then I checked the date it was posted—over a year ago.

As more questions about the Eberts buzzed around in my head, I picked up my cell and tapped on Maddie's cell phone number. If Colleen worked at the hospital, Maddie would know. I hoped she was up to answering some questions. Tobias answered my call on the second ring.

After we greeted each other, he said, "I'm screening her calls. Condolence calls started coming in before she finished her first cup of coffee. The word spread fast at the hospital. Some wanted all the details."

"Poor Maddie. I had planned to ask her a few questions, but I'll hold off until tomorrow."

"No. Maddie wants to help if it gets you closer to finding Sheila's killer. Someone drugged her."

"Maddie's convinced that's what happened?"

"Absolutely."

"Can I talk to her?"

"As soon as she gets out of the shower. You can start by asking me the questions. Maddie tells me almost everything that goes on at the hospital. I might know some of the answers."

"Does Colleen Ebert work there?"

"Not for more than twenty years, but she's kept up all the requirements to maintain her license. Rumors have been going around that she intends to return. Their son is now in college, and apparently she wants to restart her career. Colleen is certified in critical care, and Maddie's boss is hoping she doesn't pick the ICU as her starting place. Word has gotten around that when Colleen worked there, her father popped around often to see how she was doing. Maddie's boss doesn't want that."

"Colleen was a lot younger then. Feister might not do that now. Any idea what Sheila thought about Colleen returning?"

"She didn't like it but didn't seem to be too worried. Jared told her he planned to move his practice to another hospital."

"That makes sense if everything he had told Sheila—leaving his wife, divorce, marrying her—was true. Did Sheila also intend to change hospitals?"

"Not until his divorce was final. Prior to that, everything would've remained secret. She wanted him to get established first at a different hospital before she made a move…. Maddie's heading this way. Any more questions?"

"Two more…Do you know the names of other nurses Jared had affairs with? And was Sheila's prior boyfriend associated with the hospital?"

"Her prior boyfriend was a banker. I don't know the answer to the other question. Here's Maddie."

"Hi, Dora."

"How are you doing?"

"Not all that good, but I need to keep my emotions intact. There's so much I need to deal with—calling the extended family, dealing with the funeral home, writing the obituary, picking out clothes for her to wear."

"Can I help with any of that?"

"No. I want you to spend your time searching for the killer. Tobias is going to help me."

"Maddie, her body might not be released right away. Drug tests might take time."

"I didn't think about that. How can I find out?"

"Start by talking to someone in the hospital morgue. If they can't give you the information, they'll be able to direct you to the right person." I figured that the medical examiner probably had already taken custody of Sheila's body.

"Tobias said you had questions."

"He answered all of them except one. Do you know the names of the other women, nurses, who had been involved with Jared?"

"Sheila mentioned someone named Georgina. No last name. But she said it wasn't really an affair—more like a one or two night stand. She isn't a nurse. She works in administration. I don't know her."

Georgina. That's not a real common name. She was probably the same Georgina in the picture on Colleen's Twitter site.

Maddie went on. "Sheila mentioned there were others. She justified Jared's behavior by saying that he and his wife never got along and that he only stayed in the marriage because of their son."

"Do you know of anyone at the hospital who didn't get along with Sheila?"

"Well, there was Vicky, a surgical nurse, and she was also a member of Jared's surgical team. They used to be good friends until Sheila started going out with Jared. Whatever happened between them, Sheila wouldn't talk about it. Maybe Vicky had a fling with Jared. But whatever it was, it doesn't matter. Vicky died over a month ago."

"How?"

"A climbing accident. Sheila was real upset about it."

"Can you think of anyone else that didn't like Sheila?"

"The woman who took Vicky's place...What's her name?" She paused. "Janice. I don't know if she didn't like Sheila, but Sheila didn't like her. I have no idea why."

"Getting back to Vicky...did she die at Feister Northwest Hospital?"

"Yes. Instead of being taken to the closest hospital, her climbing partner, a close relative, insisted she be taken to Feister. She was helicoptered in. Do you think there's a connection?"

"I'm not leaving any stone unturned. What's Vicky's last name?"

"Marsh. Anymore questions?"

"Oh, I do have one more. Where's Jared's medical office?"

"His practice is in the medical building right next to the hospital. The two buildings are connected by an enclosed bridge."

"Is Sheila's doctor also there?"

"Yes. Dr. Mary Gransky."

"To get Sheila's medical records, I'll need your power of attorney. Are you okay with that?"

"Why do you need her medical records?"

"In case she had some condition that required her to take prescriptions. Sometimes people accidentally overdose themselves."

"Sheila didn't take any prescriptions. Oh, she did take birth control pills."

"I still want a copy of her hospital medical record when she was admitted last night."

"You can have my power of attorney if it helps."

"Are you still at Tobias's apartment?"

"Yes, but we're getting ready to leave for my house...and Sheila won't be there." Maddie's voice cracked.

"Dora, anything else?" Tobias asked as Maddie sniffled in the background.

"If I send a notary to Maddie's house, do you think she'd be up to signing a couple of documents?"

While waiting for him to respond, I heard mumbled voices. Then he replied, "Yes."

"I'll see if I can get someone there within the hour."

Chapter 4

A couple of hours later, I had the signed document and drove toward the hospital. When I stopped at a red light, my cell rang and Tucker's name appeared on the screen. "Hey."

"Forget to tell me something?" His tone was cool.

Lindgren must have mentioned seeing me the prior night. The light changed to green, and I moved along with the traffic. "You were having such a good time playing poker I didn't want to spoil it. I take it you've heard that Sheila Wilson was hit by a car and died."

"Dee, no poker game was going on this morning," he huffed.

He said that in a whole sentence—not a good sign. "I didn't want to spoil the time we had together."

"The morgue?"

"Maddie was having a hard time believing Sheila was dead. I went to the morgue to confirm her death."

"Is that all?"

"Sort of." I wanted to say "Yes." Sometimes I left things out, but I never lied to Tucker.

"Yeah. Okay. I see. Maddie doesn't buy that it was an accident."

"Was it?"

"Need to go." He clicked off.

That was unexpected. I had anticipated that he would tell me to let the police finish their job without me getting in their way, not hang up. *Tucker must really be mad.* Still, I felt irritated that he had hung up without answering my question.

Suddenly, the new investigation Grover had assigned to me, scheduled to start on Monday, bounced into my head. Thinking I might need to do some fast talking to get out of it, I cut to the curb, parked, and placed a call to Grover. It went straight to his voice mail. I left a lengthy message about looking into the death of Maddie's aunt. Grover knew Maddie, but he had never met Sheila.

When I got to the hospital, I followed signs to the medical records department. Even with the power of attorney and proof that Maddie was her next of kin, the clerk still seemed hesitant to provide me with a copy of Sheila's medical record with last night's admittance. The clerk didn't look older than twenty, and I figured she had never dealt with a power of attorney before. Eventually, I convinced her that it was legit. Like most records these days, they were electronic.

While she punched in her password, I intensely watched and memorized each stroke. Once she passed the sign-in screen, she began clicking on her keyboard numerous times. I pulled out my small notepad and scribbled down her password. A friend had been teaching me some hacking skills, but until I had those mastered, I grabbed passwords whenever I could. Sometimes they were a necessity to obtain important information in an investigation, and I didn't work under the same ethical rules as Tucker. No police protocol. No warrants.

Tilting her head, she looked at me. "You are spelling Wilson W...i...l...s...o...n?"

"Yes."

"And the first name is Sheila S...h...e...i...l...a?"

"Yes. Is there a problem?"

"There's no record of a Sheila Wilson being admitted to this hospital last night."

"She was hit by a car in the street right in front of the hospital, and she died while being prepped for surgery. Maybe you don't have the record yet."

"It comes to us through the computer system the minute she's admitted. A patient's record continues being updated while they're in the hospital."

"Who could remove it?"

"We have a security system in place that prevents that from happening."

"Obviously, your security system isn't foolproof. Sheila Wilson was a patient at your hospital last night. I was here when she was wheeled in, and I saw her body in the morgue."

The clerk shrugged.

"Who would you suggest I talk to about the lack of a medical record?"

"Sheila Wilson was not a patient in this hospital last night. If you have any complaints about the service we provide, you can discuss that with administration." She gave me directions to that department.

Walking away, I figured the newer employees were assigned to work on weekends. The twenty-year-old probably needed more training. I doubted a medical record for Sheila didn't exist, but that gave me an excuse to visit the administration department, and hopefully Georgina worked on Saturdays. If she was the same woman in the picture Colleen posted on Twitter, she would have only worked for the hospital a year. She would probably be one of the newer employees in that department and given work hours no one else wanted.

Entering the administration department, I glanced around. Several doors surrounding the room were closed. I smiled inwardly when I saw the woman from the Twitter photo sitting behind a desk.

She stood up. "May I help you?"

Clearly displayed on her blazer was a badge—Georgina Levin. She was an average-sized woman, not heavy, with shoulder-length brown hair, thinner and much more attractive in person than she appeared in the photo. She was stylishly dressed in a straight navy-blue skirt, white silk blouse, and a navy-blue blazer. A pair of navy-blue stilettos completed the outfit.

"Yes. I went to the medical records department to obtain the record for Sheila Wilson." I noticed Georgina flinch. "But the clerk couldn't find any record for her. Sheila Wilson was admitted last night right after being struck by a car."

Georgina cleared her throat. "Are you sure that Miss Wilson was admitted to this hospital?"

"Yes. I followed the gurney in."

"And why do you want her medical record?"

"For personal reasons."

"Are you related to the deceased Miss Wilson?"

Georgina knew Sheila was dead. I mentioned she had been in an accident, but not that she had died and nothing about Sheila's death had appeared in the newspaper yet. Had Georgina been keeping tabs on Jared's girlfriend? After enjoying his company for a one or two night stand, was she pining for him? "No, but I have power of attorney from her niece, Madilyn Wilson, and a document showing she is Sheila's next-of-kin in order to obtain the record."

"If Sheila Wilson was admitted to this hospital, there would be a medical record."

"Since it couldn't be located in the records department, where would I be able to obtain it?"

"The records' manager doesn't work on weekends. I'll have her search for it on Monday and contact you. Would you prefer she call you, text you, or send an email when she's located it?" She grabbed a notepad and pen and prepared to write down my information.

"So there is no way I can obtain it before Monday?"

"I'm afraid not."

"You're telling me there is no one in this hospital that has access to that medical record?"

Her eyes bore into mine. "That's right."

"Is Dr. Feister in? He is the president of this place, isn't he?"

"He is the CEO, and he's seldom in the hospital on weekends."

"Then you'll have the pleasure of seeing me again on Monday." I turned on my heel and marched out.

On my way to the ER, I put my cell on vibrate. As

I followed a nurse through the double doors, she glanced over her shoulder at me but didn't say anything. Maybe she thought I was a relative of a patient. I looked around and saw an unattended old man sleeping in a room. Pretending to be his relative, I went in, closed the door behind me, and headed to the hospital computer on a stand in the corner. Using the clerk's password, I tapped into the hospital patient records. Before I located Sheila's record, voices drifted into the room. It sounded like people were talking next to the door.

Thinking someone could enter any second, I clicked out of the system, sank down onto the chair by the bed, and took the old man's hand.

The door opened and a man in his forties, wearing a white lab coat walked in. His eyes shot to me. "Who are you?"

I couldn't see a badge on his lab coat but assumed he was a doctor. "His granddaughter."

Not questioning me, the doctor said, "When he wakes up, he can go home. Is your grandmother still in the hospital?"

"I haven't seen her since I got here, but she wouldn't go home without grandpa," I said, hoping *grandma* wouldn't show up soon.

"Have her stop by the nurses' station when she comes back."

I nodded.

He left, closing the door behind him.

I hurried back to the computer. It didn't take long before I reached Sheila Wilson's hospital medical records. I scrolled to the right date and clicked on her admittance record, a record the young clerk in the records department couldn't locate. Nothing but the date, time, and that Sheila had been hit by a car appeared on the record. Then I looked for Vicky Marsh's record. No Vicky Marsh. There was one for a Victoria Marsh. Glancing over it, I saw she had been admitted as a result of a rock climbing accident on July 30th. Her ER doctor was listed as April Holbrook. Victoria Marsh died on her way to surgery.

Hearing the door opening, I quickly got out of the hospital system.

"Who are you?" a nicely dressed, elderly woman asked.

"I'm a computer technician checking to make sure this device is properly functioning. My work here is done." I strolled toward the door. "Your husband's doctor would like you to stop by the nurses' station."

"I'll do that right now before he wakes up." The woman walked out the door behind me.

Wondering if Georgina had told the truth that Feister wasn't in or if she was just screening his visitors, I decided to pay her another visit. A male voice flowed out the open door of the administration department as I approached. Thinking Feister could be the guy talking, I slowed my pace and perked up my ears.

"...with Sheila," a man said. His baritone voice sounded too young to belong to a seventy-something Feister.

"Yes, but...Jared, this isn't a good place to talk," Georgina said.

"Agreed. Meet me at Tilly's."

On a prior investigation, I had met a client at Tilly's. It was a dive about five miles out of town. Not a place I would have expected Jared to even know about, let alone frequent.

Georgina replied, "It has to be right after work. The kids are having a sleep over tonight."

"Five-thirty."

I turned toward the wall and rummaged through my purse, expecting him to walk out the door and move down the hallway behind me. Out of the corner of my eye, I saw Jared, wearing a lab coat, going the opposite direction.

When he was out of sight, I pulled a bug out of a special compartment in my purse and felt irritated that the one I had taken with me only had a 300 foot range which meant I couldn't listen at home. Then I proceeded through the administrative department's open door.

Georgina stood by a file cabinet, thumbing through a folder. An annoyed expression flashed on her face the minute she saw me. "Like I mentioned earlier, Dr. Feister won't be in until Monday. Is there something else I can help you with?"

Moving closer to her, I *accidentally* tripped and bumped into her, dropping the bug in her blazer pocket in the process. "Sorry."

Her eyes narrowed. "What is it you want?"

"I came back to find out what time the records manager will be here on Monday morning."

"Eight-thirty a.m."

"Thank you." I smiled and left.

Before leaving the hospital, I checked my phone and saw two missed calls, a text, and a voice message. One of the calls and the text were from Tobias. His text read: "Call me." The other call and voice message came from Grover.

I took a seat and clicked on the message. Grover said he could make arrangements for someone else to cover my scheduled investigation and told me not to hesitate using any of his resources that might help in investigating Maddie's aunt's death. Feeling relieved that Grover didn't have a problem giving me time off to work on the Sheila case, I placed a call to Tobias.

When he answered, I asked, "Is something wrong?"

"Yes. Maddie called the hospital morgue. She was told the mortuary could come and pick up the body, and then she asked if a tox test had been performed. The pathologist told her it had. Since she couldn't confirm her identity over the phone, he wouldn't give her the results. Then she called her supervisor. Sheila's medical record only shows that she was admitted. No results of any testing. Her supervisor contacted a friend in the pathology department. The toxicology report shows no drugs in Sheila's blood. Maddie thinks that somehow blood samples were mixed up or someone switched them on purpose."

Pressing the phone against my ear with my shoulder, I scribbled notes as I spoke. "Sheila swayed while she walked toward the road. No drugs in her system? I don't buy it. Why wasn't the tox report, even if it was fraudulent, entered into Sheila's medical record? And why weren't any of her vitals, the name of the doctor assigned to her, or the planned surgery in her record? Tell Maddie I'll get to the bottom of it."

"Thanks, Dora. Maddie has complete confidence in you. She told me that you've solved every case that's come your way. What should she do about the body?"

"Have a mortuary pick up Sheila's body and put it in their refrigeration unit without embalming it. She can tell the mortuary that some friends and relatives will be coming from a distance, so the funeral might be a couple of weeks away. Something like that."

After the call ended, I thought about Stan Lindgren. Why had a detective been called in? When I asked Tucker if it was an accident, why didn't Tucker just tell me that was how it appeared? Even if the tox test results were accurate, which I doubted, was there another reason Sheila's death seemed suspicious?

Pleased with myself for having the foresight to collect a sample of Sheila's blood, I glanced at my watch—3:30 p.m. Since I had time to kill before Georgina got off work, I decided to go home and pick up a few long-range bugs.

Chapter 5

When I returned to the hospital parking lot to wait for Georgina to head out to Jared's rendezvous, I called my contact at the DMV and asked him what type of a car was registered under the name Georgina Levin. He found two. Both of the registrations also had a man's name on them that I took to be her husband. One car was a late-model blue Lexus coupe. The other was a black Cadillac Escalade. He gave me the license plate numbers.

I climbed out of my car and searched for Georgina's. I stopped by an Escalade at the end of my row. The license plate wasn't a match. After going up and down numerous rows, I finally found her blue Lexus on the other side of the building. Glancing at my watch—4:56 p.m., I hurried back to my car and drove it to a slot where I had a good view of her Lexus but not so close that she could easily see me.

Within five minutes, I spotted her heading toward

her car. When she drove to the parking lot exit, I pulled out my listening device, flipped it on, and pushed the button associated with the bug I'd planted in Georgina's blazer pocket. Music came through the speaker. Since I knew the location of Tilly's, I didn't need to be right on her tail, but I wanted to stay within the 300 feet transmission range so I could hear if she placed or received a call in case the meeting location had changed.

Georgina made a call. A young female voice came through the airwaves. Georgina told her that she needed to run a few errands on her way home. I assumed the voice belonged to one of Georgina's children.

Then I noticed a gray Volvo in the next lane and recalled seeing a car just like it leaving the hospital parking lot right before I did. As I continued listening to Georgina's music, I stopped at a red light three cars behind her and almost even with the gray Volvo. The driver was a woman with light brown hair styled in a bob that hit right below her ears. From my angle, I couldn't see her face.

When the light changed, I slowly accelerated and glanced at the Volvo's license plate. Oregon. I was able to catch the first three numbers and one alpha.

Cars were parked along the curb in front of Tilly's, taking every available spot. Georgina pulled down a lane next to it. The gray Volvo eased by the cars. I double parked for a few minutes to give Georgina enough time to park and go inside.

"Over here." Jared's voice streamed through the listening device.

They greeted each other as I drove down the lane. Cars filled about half of the good-sized lot. I backed into a parking space. I'd be prepared to quickly leave if I decided to follow her or Jared.

"I ordered your usual," Jared said.

I stepped out of my car and scanned the parking lot for Jared's Porsche. A white one was parked five spaces from me. I took a long-range bug out of my purse and headed toward that vehicle, hoping it was Jared's. To me, he was the key to Sheila's death. Picking up anything he said might be helpful. Then I began checking the windows to see if there was a way I could squeeze the bug in. Moving around the car, I smiled when I saw the passenger window was slightly ajar and pushed the bug through the opening. It slid down between the bucket seat and the door. Since I couldn't see exactly where it landed, there was a chance it could fall out when someone opened the passenger door. Still, if I obtained even a little bit of information before that happened, losing the bug would be worth it.

Scooting behind the steering wheel, I heard Georgina say, "not be her."

"She's my best guess," Jared said. "Have you got a better one?"

"No. How did you fix the blood tests?" Georgina's voice was just above a whisper.

I turned up the volume on my listening device.

"I didn't. I think it was her."

I stared at the listening device. Who is "her"? I shook my head, mad at myself. I should have listened and waited to attempt to plant a bug in Jared's car when their conversation indicated they were ready to leave.

"And the detective?" Georgina asked.

"From what Martin said…"

"Who's Martin?"

"Martin Tidman, the pathologist who met the accident investigator and the detective in the morgue. According to Martin, the detective wasn't assigned to check out anything to do with the accident. He was visiting a friend at the hospital and accompanied the accident investigator to the morgue. He wasn't on duty."

"That's good. I still don't understand how Sheila could have found out about that night."

"Sheila wasn't a threat. She would've kept it a secret to protect me....What am I going to do?" Jared's voice sounded heavy with despair. "I want justice for Sheila."

"Jared, I'm sorry for your loss," Georgina said in a soft, soothing voice. "But you can't tell anyone."

"I know. I'd probably lose my license and everyone who was there will suffer consequences, especially..."

"Don't even think about it." Georgina lowered her voice again.

Turning up the listening device even more, I missed a few words.

"...police isn't an option...do you think she harbors resentment against all of us?"

"She was in complete agreement. How to dispose of...was her plan. And she was..."

"If she's responsible for Sheila—I'm still not convinced it was her—she might have gone after her because she thought Sheila would squeal. She'll want to know who told Sheila. We could all be in danger."

I recalled Jared saying to Sheila in the morgue, "I never should have told you." Was that regarding the night they were discussing?

"I've left several messages on Malcolm's phone," Jared said. "He hasn't returned any of my calls. Have you talked to him about Sheila?"

"No. Since he moved out, he only speaks to me when it has something to do with the kids. If I even mention the cabin, he clams right up. Telling him about Sheila might be too much for him to handle."

"Like the rest of us, he's probably trying to wipe out the whole day...pretend it never happened."

"Malcolm never wanted to go. He's blaming me for dragging him there. But until that night, he was having a good time. Sometimes the cabin thing creeps into my dreams. I'll never set a foot anywhere around that place again....I need to get home to the kids."

"Just in case, watch your back," Jared said. "Don't eat or drink anything she gives you."

"Oh, there's some woman snooping around. She has Sheila's niece's power of attorney and wants Sheila's medical records."

"Let her have them. Now there's nothing in them that would raise any suspicion."

As I listened to muffled voices and the clicking sound of high heels striking a hard surface, I sank further down in my seat. No one walking by my car would be able to see me through the front windshield.

I ran the conversation through my head. What could have happened that night that would cause consequences for everyone present? And threaten Jared's license? Illegal recreational drugs? Someone overdosed? Could Jared have performed some kind of illegal operation that went badly? What's an illegal operation? Abortions were legal, but was there a requirement they must be performed in a medical facility? Why would any licensed doctor not do it in a proper facility? And I couldn't imagine a renowned cardiac surgeon even consider doing that type of procedure. And what did they dispose that night? A body?

From what I gathered from their conversation, the list of prime suspects I had started was probably wrong. It was based on the premise the person responsible did it because Sheila was the other woman—one of Jared's former lovers who still yearned to be with him...or a betrayed wife? I wasn't ready to completely rule them out, but the case had just taken on a new twist. I needed to find out about that night. Whatever went down might have caused someone to kill to keep it a secret.

Hearing music and the sound of traffic coming through the listening device, I knew Georgina had pulled out of the parking lot. Suddenly, when the noise stopped coming through the device, I thought about the gray Volvo and sat up straight. As I drove out of the parking lot, I noticed the white Porsche hadn't budged. Since there was a long-range bug in that vehicle, I pushed the button on the listening device that went to that bug.

I merged into the traffic and headed the direction the Volvo had gone. A gray Volvo was parked a short distance from Tilly's. The first four digits of the license plate were the same as the Volvo I suspected earlier was following Georgina. Did the driver not know that she had left Tilly's? Or was the car not following her at all?

Since I was so busy looking at the license plate when I drove by, I never noticed if a person was in the vehicle. At my first opportunity, I flipped a U-ey. The driver, a female, leaned against the steering wheel with her head tilted toward the passenger seat. So I couldn't see her face. Did she know Georgina planned to meet Jared but didn't know where? Could that be it? Was she here because of Jared? Or was she here for an entirely different reason? I made a mental note to call my DMV contact in the morning. With the model of the car and the first four digits of the license plate, there was a strong possibility that he could find the owner in the system.

The rumbling sound of a car engine blared through the listening device.

Figuring Jared had started his car, I pulled over to the curb, wanting to see if the Volvo followed the Porsche. Within five minutes, the Porsche sped past me. A minute later, the Volvo went by. Someone was keeping tabs on Jared. *Who? And why?*

I cut into the traffic, intending to tail the Volvo. The light turned red before I reached the intersection. While I waited, the tail lights of the Volvo faded in the distance. Hoping to catch up to it, I gunned my engine and zoomed away from the intersection the second the light changed. The Volvo was nowhere in sight.

Deciding to call it a night, I pulled into a parking lot and set my listening device to record, voice-activated. Since Georgina's bug only had a 300 foot range, I knew I wouldn't be able to pick up anything from that bug. Even getting something meaningful from the one in Jared's car was remote, but the possibility did exist. I intended to find a way to plant a bug on him, though I didn't have a clue where I could put one that would stay with him for most of the day and night. Why didn't men carry purses with them? Bugging women was so much easier.

Chapter 6

When I turned the corner, I saw Tucker's car in the driveway. Even though, I didn't want to deal with him confronting me about snooping around the morgue, I really needed to know what the police found out about Sheila's death.

The minute I opened the door, the wonderful aroma of garlic and spiced meat floated through the air. Tucker stepped out of the kitchen. "Want a glass of wine before dinner?"

Was he trying to make up to me for hanging up? "Yes, I'd like that." I strolled toward him and peeked into the kitchen. Looking at the counter, I saw remnants of vegetables, cheese, and pasta. In the corner sat a plate filled with chocolate chip cookies, my favorite. "Is today some kind of special occasion that I've forgotten about?"

"No," he said, handing me a wine goblet. "Just cheering up time."

I took a sip of wine. "And why do I need to be cheered up?"

"Sheila's accident."

Leaning against the door frame, I watched Tucker take a cooking dish filled with lasagna out of the fridge and put it in the oven while I drank more wine. "The tox report came back negative. Suicide was ruled out. The accident investigator concluded it was an accident."

"Suicide? Sheila would never consider that."

"Like I said, suicide was ruled out." A crease formed between Tucker's eyes as he gazed at me. "That's confidential and so is the tox report."

"I have Maddie's power of attorney to obtain Sheila's medical records," I said, though that wasn't how I got the results. "And the tox report is inaccurate. It wasn't Sheila's blood that was tested."

Tucker grabbed a bottle of beer out of the fridge, opened it, and took a swig. "Dee, are you planning to make the police department look bad again?" He used a business-like tone, and a full sentence signaled this was an interrogation.

"That only happened once."

He cocked his head.

"Okay, twice."

"Dee?"

This case is more complicated than I anticipated. I could use Tucker's help since I couldn't exactly ask Grover to assign another investigator to assist me on a pro-bono case. "Okay...okay, maybe it was more than that, but I didn't set out to make the department look bad. You and I both know those cases were no longer being worked. And now you're telling me there won't be a criminal case opened about Sheila's death. Well, I know she was drugged before she left the hospital. She staggered to the street. I saw that with my own eyes. On top of that, she left her purse in the hospital along with her raincoat, and it was raining. So the police department is almost forcing me to make them look bad again."

"The blood in the test tube that you hid in the fridge at the back of a vegetable drawer—you took that from Sheila?"

He'd caught me, I couldn't lie to him. "Yes. Right before I bumped into Stan Lindgren in the hospital."

"That explains why you were wearing a nurse's uniform." He came closer to me and put his arm around my shoulder. Sensing my question, he said, "Of course he remembered you. You're a knockout. I hadn't planned to work this evening, but you've piqued my curiosity. Let's sit on the couch, and you can tell me what you've got."

Gazing at his dark hazel eyes, I said, "Is this how you treat everyone that comes to you with a scoop?"

He pulled me closer to him and kissed my forehead. "How'd you know?" A mischievous smile crossed his face. "You spying on me?"

"Every chance I get."

As I started to brief Tucker about Sheila's hospital medical records, or lack thereof, the timer on the oven buzzed.

Tucker stood up. "Just turning it off. It'll stay warm in the oven."

"I'm starving, and it smells so good. We can come back to this after dinner."

Tucker and I had a rule that we never discussed our work when we ate in the dining room. He filled our wine glasses and then served the lasagna with garlic bread. He joked about one of his poker buddies moaning over losing twenty bucks. That was pittance compared to what a couple of the other guys lost. But they were all anxious for another poker night, convinced they'd win everything back.

After we finished dinner and cleaned-up, I filled him in about the conversation between Jared and Georgina and the gray Volvo that had followed Jared when he left the bar.

"You bugged them."

"Yep. I know it's illegal, but I can't go around flashing a badge to get information like you can. Even with a badge, neither Jared nor Georgina would tell any detective that Sheila's death was more than an accident. But from what they said, neither of them was responsible for the negative toxicology report. Jared wants justice for Sheila, but he can't come forward without talking about "that night.""

"Did you record it?"

I pressed my lips together and shook my head. "No."

"Without a recording, they'd both deny everything they said in the bar. It would be a 'he said, she said' kind of thing. Do you have any concrete evidence?"

I narrowed my lips. "The blood. Would that be enough for you to open a case?"

"I'll have it tested. Even though it was acquired illegally, maybe if the results come back positive, I can convince Fred to let me work on the case." Sergeant Fred Shoeman was Tucker's boss.

"No, I'll have it tested and give you the results."

"You don't trust me to take care of it?"

"I trust you, but Raymond Feister has a lot of connections in this town—probably contacts in the police department—and his daughter is a nurse. I haven't ruled out that Colleen could be responsible, and if she is, then he might try to suppress the result."

Tucker stroked my cheek. "You're assuming Feister would know about it."

"Until Sheila's murderer is found, everyone at Feister Northwest Hospital is a suspect."

"You're calling it murder?"

"Damn straight. It might not be that in the eyes of the law, but to Maddie it is. Had Sheila not been drugged she never would've wandered out into the traffic. In addition to locating the culprit, maybe I can find some evidence that the person intended to kill her. The black sedan just beat them to it." I took a sip of wine. "What would be the point of drugging her if the guilty party didn't have other plans for her? Different scenarios keep running through my mind. Maybe that person anticipated to meet up with her when she was away from the hospital and shoot her up with more drugs so she'd die from an overdose. Doing that in the hospital could be risky for anyone associated with it—like a doctor or nurse. In Sheila's condition, she couldn't have gone far. It would've been easy for someone to catch up with her. She stopped and looked back at the hospital. Was she expecting someone to come after her? Was she attempting to get away from that person when she walked out into the street?

"Jared and Georgina also talked like Sheila's death wasn't an accident. And they've seen the real tox report. Maybe there's something more there."

"I think it'll be easier for me to convince Fred to let me work on the case if the toxicology screening is done by the medical examiner. No name will be put on the test tube. It'd be identified by a number."

I sighed. "Okay. Then take it tomorrow and have it tested." Since it had not been legally acquired and I lacked proof that the blood belonged to Sheila, I knew it could never be used as evidence. In order to bring the case forward, I needed legally obtained evidence even if I learned about it through illegal means. "With your workload, would you even have time to work on the case?"

"From what you've told me, it appears there is a strong possibility that whatever went down that night at a cabin someplace, a crime was committed that involved a group of people. Working on Sheila Wilson's case might give us the answer."

"What do you think would cause Jared to worry about losing his license?"

"An illegal operation? Covering up a crime? My guess would be a gunshot wound."

"Right. Doctors are required to report them. Gunshot wound. That never entered my mind probably because I couldn't envision any of Jared's friends or associates packing."

"Enough business talk." He wrapped his arms around me and smothered my lips with his.

My skin tingled with anticipation as he took my hand and led me into the bedroom. All thoughts about Sheila's case vanished when Tucker started unbuttoning my blouse.

Chapter 7

After my morning cup-of-Joe, I called Maddie.

"Hey," she answered. "Have you learned anything?"

"It's moving along. How are you doing today?"

"Much better. Tobias treats me like I might break any minute. He cooks all the meals, made all the arrangements with the mortuary, wrote Sheila's obituary, and called my relatives. I don't have many, but it was sweet of him to take care of that. He even called most of Sheila's friends. Those that called me, I ended up talking to. They'll all need to be called back once we have a funeral date."

"Are you up to answering a few more questions?"

"Yes. I want to see Sheila's killer behind bars."

"How long had Sheila been having an affair with Jared?"

"Let me think…over six months. We fought about it all the time. Jared's married. Sheila's never fallen for a married man before. Well, she did once, but that guy was in the process of getting a divorce. He didn't live with his wife."

"Has she ever mentioned anything about a cabin?"

Maddie sighed. "Oh, yes. Colleen's family has one. I have no idea where it is. A month or so ago, Jared went there with Colleen for a weekend. Sheila was furious."

"Just the two of them?"

"No. It was to celebrate April's birthday—her fortieth."

"Is April a close friend?"

"She's Colleen's sister."

From everything I had read, I thought Colleen was an only child. "Does Colleen have other siblings?" I asked

"No. Just April."

"Does April work at the hospital?" I asked, recalling the name April Holbrook on Victoria Marsh's medical record.

"Yes. She's an ER doc and just as nice as can be. Sheila and April often went to lunch together."

"That's cozy—she's having an affair with April's sister's husband and still maintaining a friendship with her."

"April was indirectly responsible for Sheila and Jared hooking up. Sheila worked on Jared's surgical team, but they had never seen each other socially until April invited Sheila to a barbeque at her place."

"Does April know about the affair?"

"I doubt it. April was the first to examine Sheila when she was rushed into the ER. We cried on each others' shoulders when…" Maddie swallowed hard.

"Oh, Maddie, maybe I should call you later."

"No." She cleared her throat. "I'm okay."

"Are you sure?"

"Yes."

"Let's get back to April's birthday party at the cabin. Besides Colleen, Jared, April, and her husband, was there anyone else there?"

"April's going through a messy divorce with her husband, Mark Holbrook. That's why they had the party at the cabin. She wanted to get away from the city, and the cabin is her favorite place. Her soon-to-be ex-husband wasn't invited. It was an adult party…no kids. I think five people went—Colleen, Jared, Georgina, her husband, but I don't know his name—and April."

"Georgina? The same woman Jared had a one-or-two-night stand with?"

"Yes. She's Colleen's and April's cousin. Their only cousin. Georgina was part of the reason Sheila was so mad about Jared going."

"Nothing like keeping it in the family. Besides being messy, do you know anything else about April's divorce?" I asked, wanting to learn more about the doctor who saw both Vicky Marsh and Sheila in the ER.

"Sheila said that April's husband had some serious mental problems. That's all I know. What does that, the cabin, or party have to do with Sheila's death?"

"I'm trying to determine everyone who might have known about Jared's affair with Sheila, and I overheard Jared mention a cabin."

"Oh, you think that might have been a place he took Sheila," Maddie said.

I wasn't ready to let her know that assumption was wrong. Until I knew more, I never revealed very much to my clients.

Maddie continued. "No way. The place would probably be off limits to him unless Colleen went with him."

"Yeah, I can't imagine Jared being bold enough to carry on an affair at a place belonging to the Feister family. Thanks for the info."

Laying down my cell, I thought about April Holbrook. Maddie had said that Vicky might've had an affair with Jared, and Sheila was his current squeeze. Could April have played a role in both deaths to help her sister? But since she was an ER doctor, there might not be a connection at all.

Then I focused on the cabin. The problem that Jared and Georgina talked about might not have occurred at the birthday party Maddie mentioned. Last night, Georgina said she'd never go there again. If it didn't happen at that party weekend, which was about a month ago, then it had taken place since then.

I tapped on my keyboard and searched for the cabin. Quickly, I located a cabin owned by the Raymond Feister Family Trust. Assuming it was the right place, I did a Google search to find approximately how long it would take me to get there—two and a half hours.

My chances of accidentally running into Jared on a Sunday to plant a bug somewhere on his clothing was nil. And Tucker was working on a homicide, but he had promised he'd have the blood tested before he came home. He had no idea when that would be. So I decided it was a perfect day for a road trip.

* * *

I put a pair of binoculars, a backpack, and snacks on my passenger seat. As a precaution, I stuck my Berretta in the glove compartment. If Sheila was killed to keep whatever went down at the cabin a secret, the killer might not hesitate to kill again for the same reason.

Driving toward the cabin, I mulled over the five people that Maddie thought had attended the birthday party. Jared referred to the person he believed was behind Sheila's death as a 'she.' Going under the assumption that the dreaded incident occurred one night during the party weekend and no one else besides those five people were there, it had to be either Colleen or April.

Jared was concerned about potentially losing his license over what had happened there. Tucker thought someone might have sustained a gunshot wound and Jared had operated on that individual but never reported it. Georgina's husband, Malcolm Levin, had left her right after that weekend. Had he sustained a gunshot wound? From the conversation I overhead between Jared and Georgina, it sounded like he had developed some emotional issues as result of that night. Neither one of them had said anything to indicate her husband had sustained an injury. Had a stranger wandered into the cabin and someone got excited and pulled a trigger? Could that be it? Shooting an intruder did sometimes happen. If that was the case, I doubt anyone would've landed in jail. Why wouldn't they have called the police? And why would Jared take care of a wounded intruder and not report it? No, there had to be more to it than that. Questions buzzed around in my head during the drive.

Following my GPS system, I left the highway and moved along a country road through a heavily wooded area. After going approximately fifteen miles, the system told me to make a right turn. I ended up on a dirt lane with cabins and small houses scattered through the trees. None of them struck me as being large enough to contain more than a couple of bedrooms. Did some of the party goers sleep on the floor? According to the description of Feister's property, it included a cabin and a ten acre parcel of land. The structures I could see were too close together.

Guessing my GPS had led me to the wrong place, I pulled over to the side of the lane into the abutting wild grasses when two kids riding bikes came down the lane. I climbed out of the car and waved them to stop.

"Need something?" the older boy, who was around twelve-years-old, asked.

"Yes. I'm looking for a cabin belonging to a family with the last name of Feister. Do you know where that cabin is?"

Both boys shook their heads.

"No," the older boy said. "Uncle Hank runs a store up the road. He might know."

"Where is that store?"

The older boy proceeded to give me directions.

"Thanks." I slid back into my car.

Jogging my car back-and-forth on the dirt lane, I finally got it turned around so the hood faced the paved country road and headed toward it. Then I drove deeper into the woods.

Within ten minutes, I parked by a convenience store. Two gas pumps sat idle in front of it. A middle-aged man with a bushy beard, who I figured was Hank, stood behind the counter, ringing up an order. When that customer left, I said, "I'm looking for a cabin that belongs to the Feister family. One of your nephews mentioned that you might know where it is."

"Sure do." Gesturing with his hand, Hank said, "Three miles up the street. Black wrought-iron gate. Can't miss it. Only place with that fancy gate. Easy to spot. You meetin' a Feister there?"

"No," I said hesitantly, wondering if he kept tabs on their place.

"When you do, remind 'em there's a no shootin' law around here. Betsy sure will call the sheriff next time guns go off at that place. Stuck a note on the gate but ain't seen any of 'em for a while."

"I'll tell them. Thanks for the directions." I left the store, thinking Tucker had probably been right. Someone had been shot. *Who?* And Hank had said "guns"—plural. Maybe they kept a supply of weapons there.

I reached the wrought-iron gate and saw a notice taped next to a padlock securing the gate to a pole. In case someone was at the cabin, I couldn't use the excuse that I had accidently driven down the wrong lane after picking the lock. I parked about a hundred feet from the gate, tucked my pistol and binoculars in my backpack, put it on, and locked my car. Dropping the keys in my pocket, I went to the gate and read the notice. The sheet was wrinkled and weathered, probably from recent rains. Most of the letters on it were badly smeared, but I could make out the date, almost a month prior, and the bolded words—NO SHOOTING ALLOWED. After that was a long paragraph with only a few readable words, not enough to figure out what it said.

Instead of using my picks to unlock the six-foot gate, I employed by acrobatic ability and scrambled over it and then maneuvered through the trees near the graveled lane. When I spotted the cabin, I stayed well-hidden in the foliage and pulled out my binoculars. Scanning the area around the cabin, I didn't see any cars or people. The front door was shut and curtains covered all the windows. The place looked deserted. A broken chair lay on the ground near the stairs leading to a porch that appeared to encircle the two-story structure. A short distance from the cabin was a lake and a fishing boat tied to a pier.

Remaining on high alert, I cautiously moved around the cabin. No cars were parked behind it. Feeling confident that no one was there, I made my way to the back door. As an extra precaution, I knocked and listened intently for any sound or movement from inside. Nothing. I picked the lock and entered. Everything looked neat and orderly in the large room. A kitchen covered the back of it. In the middle was a large table surrounded by eight chairs. A stone fireplace dominated one wall. A stairwell and two closed doors were on the opposite wall. Two couches, three cushioned chairs, and end tables occupied the space near the fireplace. Paintings of farm animals adorned the walls. No family pictures. Frilly curtains decorated the windows. It was a modestly furnished cabin of the uber-rich. Something about it didn't feel right.

One of the closed doors led to a bathroom. A bedroom was behind the other closed door. No bedding was on the bed. The mattress appeared new.

I went into that room and briefly looked through bureau drawers. They only contained clothing. Coats and casual clothing hung in the closet. Hiking boots, rubber boots, and a couple of pairs of athletic shoes were on the floor. Next to the closet was another bathroom. I rummaged through it but nothing in it struck me as being unusual.

Then I headed upstairs, wandered through the hallway, and saw four bedrooms. Walking into each one, I noticed they all had a bathroom attached. All the beds were made, ready for visitors. A few of the drawers held clothing but most were empty.

Wondering if the Feisters had a cleaning crew that always kept the place looking this good, I ran my fingers over the top of the bureau in the last bedroom. Dust. Then I backtracked to the other bedrooms and bathrooms upstairs. They all had settled dust on the furniture and countertop. I doubted if anyone had been there since the notice had been attached to the gate.

A car engine roared outside.

I hurried to the front upstairs bedroom and peeked around the curtain. Coming down the lane was a gray Volvo. Was that the same car that followed Jared last night? A brown-haired, slender woman climbed out and walked toward the porch.

I slowly moved to the door and pushed it, leaving it ajar. Then I crept back to the window, unlocked it, and slightly opened it. To my chagrin, it had a screen. Then I closed and locked it.

The front cabin door squeaked open.

Stealthily, I eased down the hallway to the next bedroom. Relieved to see that no screen was on the window, I quietly unlocked it, pushed it up, and stuck my head out. From the ledge, I only had to jump four feet to reach the sloped roof over the porch. A screen lay on top of it. *Have any of the Feisters climbed out this window?* I lowered the window, leaving just enough to slip my fingers under it. In case the new arrival wandered around outside and looked at the cabin, she wouldn't be able to detect that the window wasn't securely closed. Then I heard the dull murmur of a voice. Thinking she was talking on a phone, I crept toward the stairs.

"...must have...No....Colleen, it had to be you. You were the one that locked up....No, nothing looks disturbed....Oh, let me check. I'll call you right back."

Footfalls on the steps echoed through the cabin.

Guessing the woman was April, I ducked into the second bedroom, the one with my escape route, and hid on the other side of the bed. Unless she entered the room and went to the window, April wouldn't be able to spot me. I doubted she was packing, and I also doubted she'd call the cops. Worst case scenario, I'd be embarrassed if she caught me in the cabin.

Clanking and banging noises drifted from the hallway. I couldn't figure out what she was up to. The noises made me curious, so I softly stepped to the door and peered between the hinges. A folding ladder was attached to the open hatch that went into the attic. April was nowhere in sight. A few seconds later, her foot landed on the top step of the ladder, and she climbed down with a striped small sack in her hand. I quietly went to the other side of the bed and hunkered down, wondering what was in the sack.

After feet pounded on the stairwell, I crept out into the hallway again to listen to her return phone call.

"I've got it....Yes....The police detective...No....Had he not called today, I wouldn't be here. I just came to pick that up and make sure everything outside looked okay....I have the perfect place to stash it....Not my place....Yes, tomorrow....I have the day off. I'll come by your house after....I'm going to put sheets and blankets on it....The broken chair is still outside. I thought you were going to take it with you. I'll dump it someplace....We all searched for it. His wallet is nowhere in the cabin. He wouldn't have left it outside. Sometimes he never carried a wallet....I'll look there....I haven't....Okay, bye."

A door downstairs opened and closed. To see if she had gone outside, I went to the bedroom at the back of the house and carefully peered out the edge of the curtain. She was walking toward the lake. She stopped a short distance from it and picked up a branch. Using it in a sweeping motion, she moved it over the dirt. Then she threw the branch on top of a wood pile and ran her hands over and through a cluster of bushes as she bent down and looked around. *Is she searching for a wallet in the bushes?*

April walked to the pier and went to the boat. She leaned forward. It appeared she was looking inside the boat, but with her back toward me, I couldn't be certain. A few minutes later, she returned to the cabin.

Hearing clanking noises of doors and cabinets opening and closing and footfalls on the wooden floor, I figured she was gathering bedding to make up the bed on the main floor, something she'd told Colleen she planned to do before leaving the cabin.

In case April intended to check all the bedrooms

and make sure the windows were locked, I decided it was time to make my exit while she was busy downstairs. I scooted out the window and lowered myself to the porch roof. In the process, my foot smacked into the side of the screen and it slid off the roof, hitting the ground with a thud.

Scurrying along the roof, I made my way to the back of the house and climbed down a pole. I heard a loud thump come from the front of the house and sprinted toward the trees. Rushing away from the graveled lane, I dashed around bushes and trees. As I leapt over the edge of a large pile of twigs and broken branches, my shoe lace caught on a limb, and I landed face down on the ground. Before standing up, I crawled around the pile to a hidden spot and brushed the dirt off of my face and hair. As I tied my shoe lace, I saw a red shiny object in the pile.

To check if April was hot on my trail, I perked up my ears and listened. All I heard was my heavy breathing and leaves blowing in the soft breeze. No pounding of feet through the foliage. Curious about the red object, I slowly removed a few branches to get to it. In the process, I discovered the branches and twigs were concealing a red Corvette. *Who hid the car? Did it have anything to do with that night?*

Pushing more branches away from the vehicle, I moved to the rear of the car to look for a license plate. When I saw it, I took a notepad out of my backpack and jotted down the number. Then I peered through the rear window. A bundle that ran the width of the interior was behind the front seats. I couldn't see anything else in the car. A horrible thought struck me. *Is there a body hidden in that bundle or is one in the trunk?* I attempted to open the trunk—locked.

To get to the car door, I threw more branches off the vehicle. As I reached the handle, the sound of a car, wheels crunching on the gravel, came from the direction of the lane. Since I had uncovered quite a bit of the car, I worried that if April looked this direction she might see something gleaming through the trees. Holding my breath, I ducked to the other side of the pile and listened. Not hearing the car slow down, I waited until the woods became quiet again.

I went back to the car door and rummaged through my backpack for anything I could use to break into the Corvette. Nothing. I hurried back to the cabin, broke in, and grabbed a few wire hangers. As I ran back toward the woods, I noticed the broken chair was gone.

Using a hanger, it only took me a few minutes to break into the vehicle. The bundle consisted of canvas tarps. No body. There was a large dark spot on the rubber, floor mat. It looked like dried oil, but I wouldn't rule out the possibility that it could be blood. Since I didn't have anything with me to test it or collect a sample, I closed the door and went to the trunk. To my relief, it only contained a tool box, a shovel, and a pick. Wondering how the Corvette driver managed to get the car through the woods, I lifted up some of the debris around the trees and found tire tracks and realized there was enough space between the trees that a car could easily be maneuvered through them.

The Corvette appeared to be a late model. Most likely, it was hidden to help cover up whatever had happened "that night," but leaving it on the Feister property was not smart. Maybe this was only a temporary spot, and the car would be moved once someone figured out what to do with it. April came to pick up the sack and check out the grounds because a detective was going to question her about her missing husband. Why wasn't she concerned about the Corvette? *Doesn't she know it's here?*

Wanting to leave the red Corvette the same way I found it, I piled branches and twigs back on it until it was completely hidden again. Then I went toward the road and scaled the six foot fence, tearing my pant leg in the process. While I walked to my car, not one car passed me on the road. I slid into the driver's seat, pulled out my cell phone, and changed it from vibrate to sound. Then I saw one missed call and one voice message. Both came from Tucker. He wanted me to return his call. I tapped on his number.

He answered after the first ring. "Hey, Dee. Lots to fill you in about. Coming home soon?"

"On my way, but it'll take me over two hours to get there."

"Why?"

"I paid a visit to Feister's cabin. Did you or another detective call April Holbrook today?"

"Yes. Stan did."

"She showed up at the cabin to collect something while I was there. She didn't see me but probably knows someone was there. I'll tell you all about my visit when I get home."

"Drive carefully."

I disconnected, flipped a U-ey, and headed home.

My eyes drifted to the closed wrought iron gate as I drove by. The notice that had been attached to it was gone.

As I mulled over my cabin visit, I couldn't understand why April had not gone searching for an intruder after hearing the loud thud of the screen smashing to the ground. Did she think the breeze in the air caused it to fall down? Then I pressed my lips together. Topnotch investigators could spy on someone without drawing attention. Knocking down the screen was not something a high-skilled investigator would've done.

Suddenly, the recorder in my listening device clicked on.

Jared's voice came through the speaker. "The patient isn't doing well. I don't know when I'll be home." A car door slammed shut.

A few minutes later he said, "I'm on my way."

A voice I recognized as belonging to Georgina said, "Thanks, Jared."

The recorder clicked off.

Chapter 8

It was almost 8:30 p.m. when I walked into my house. Tucker warmed up leftover lasagna while I showered and changed into a pair of sweats.

While I ate in the kitchen so we wouldn't break the "no business talking in the dining room" rule, Tucker grabbed a beer out of the fridge and began. "A month ago, on August 21st, April Feister Holbrook reported her estranged husband, Mark, missing. He was supposedly going to take their child, a seven-year-old boy, to a baseball game on August 18th, but he never showed up to pick up the kid. She tried reaching him by phone. No answer. He lives in a secure apartment building. She went there. He never answered the intercom. At his place of employment, she was told he had left for a vacation. His parents and a few friends told her the same thing. According to her, Mark Holbrook wouldn't have blown off his son. They'd been talking about the game for a week. She also said that Holbrook had been going through bouts of severe depression. She was concerned that he might not be taking his medication. She didn't know the name of his psychiatrist. "

Tucker took a swig of his beer and then continued. "The desk officer made some calls. Holbrook's phone immediately went to voicemail. He left a message. Holbrook's parents were contacted. They said that their son had been having a hard time since being separated from his wife and son. He wanted to get away to clear his head and had flown to Paris. Some of his college friends lived there. They thought he'd be gone two or three weeks. Holbrook's parents had only told his wife that he had taken a trip. When they were asked about his depression, they almost hissed and said it was just something April made up to justify kicking him out. They believed the whole separation was April's fault, and they didn't have a kind word to say about her.

"April Holbrook was given an update. It was assumed the missing person's report had no merit and no further action was done at that time. Last week, three weeks after the filing of the missing person's report, April Holbrook came into the police station again and said her estranged husband was still missing. He never returned from any trip. During that time, she claimed she had tried to call him numerous times and left messages. His boss had called her the day before looking for him. He had only been scheduled to be off work for two weeks.

"The desk officer made some calls. Holbrook's employer confirmed what April had told him. Holbrook's parents said they hadn't heard from him but not hearing from their son for a couple of months wasn't unusual."

"Where do his parents live?" I asked between bites.

"Florida. The case was turned over to Stan. He's talked to his boss, relatives, some of the other tenants in the building, and some of his friends in Paris. Holbrook's parents gave him the numbers. Holbrook never called or made arrangements to see any of them. No record of Holbrook booking a flight can be found. His apartment has been searched for any information that might lead to his whereabouts. Nothing. Stan's obtained a subpoena to obtain Holbrook's cell phone records from his provider.

"I've discussed Sheila Wilson with him. He contacted April Holbrook to set up an appointment with her. Stan intends to give her an update and do a more extensive interview. Since April Holbrook also knew Sheila, I'm going to sit in on the interview."

"Mark's disappearance might flow right into what I saw and heard while visiting Feister's cabin." I grabbed my notepad out of my backpack, tore out the page that contained the red Corvette's license, and handed it to him. "I discovered a red Corvette hidden under a pile of branches and twigs as I escaped from the cabin. Can you find out who owns it?" I filled my wine glass.

"Escaping from the cabin? What happened?" he said, pulling his cell phone out of his pocket.

"I'll tell you all about it after you make the call."

Tucker strolled out of the kitchen as he placed the call.

As he chatted on his phone, I sipped wine and tried to listen, but I only picked up a few words.

"It belongs to April Holbrook," he said, walking

back into the kitchen.

"Huh? I thought it was Mark's car."

"Even if she owns it, it might be the car that Mark drives." He took another beer out of the fridge. "Now tell me why you had to escape."

I proceeded to fill him in from the chat with the store owner, Hank, to climbing out the cabin window.

"How big was the sack she took out of the attic?"

"Small. April came to make sure the grounds looked okay and to pick that up because a detective had called her about Mark Holbrook. My guess would be illegal drugs or a small pistol."

He tented his fingers and tapped them together. "Sweeping the dirt? That would indicate something is buried in that area. I can't get a search warrant without showing probable cause a crime had been committed there. You suspect something went on there through illegal means—bugging people, trespassing, and breaking into a cabin. Nothing I can take to Fred."

"What about the hidden car?"

"You saw that when you were illegally trespassing."

"No one would hide a late model Corvette if something fishy hadn't gone on."

"Agreed. But even with your illegal bugging, you haven't picked up anyone mentioning a Corvette. Hiding it might not have had anything to do with that night. Like you, I suspect it does, but I need to discover it through a search warrant. Were you able to check inside the car and the trunk?"

"Yes. In the back area inside the car was a bundle of canvas tarps. On the front mat—passenger side—there was a dark stain. I didn't have anything with me to check if it was blood. Trunk—no body. Just tools, shovel, and a pick."

"Shovel and a pick? Any signs of blood on them?"

"No. They still had store labels on them, like they had just been purchased. Oh, on the way home, I overheard Jared saying he was going to Georgina's this evening. He lied to someone, probably his wife, saying he had to check on a patient." I gave Tucker a smile, knowing he didn't approve of me planting bugs, or maybe he did, but since that was against police procedures he always rolled his eyes whenever I mentioned overhearing something.

"Well, you already know the guy cheats on his wife."

"Yes, but when he called her to say he was on his way, Georgina thanked him. To me, that didn't sound like they were going to hook up. It sounded more like she wanted to talk to him about a problem. What do you think?"

"You could be right." He took my hand. "Or she's desperate to get him in her bed."

"They did have a one-or-two night stand, and she is separated from her husband. Okay, I get it. I almost forgot…what about the blood test?"

Tucker rubbed his chin. "Drugs were found in the blood. Since the results contradict those provided by the hospital, and I couldn't provide any proof that the blood came from Sheila Wilson, the medical examiner wants access to her body. Her body is no longer at the hospital. It was picked up by a mortuary yesterday."

"I know. The body was released after the negative tox test. Maddie had a mortuary pick it up. Sheila's body is being kept in the mortuary's refrigeration unit.

Not embalmed."

"Good. We'll need permission from Maddie to obtain it."

"That won't be a problem. It'll probably be better if you contact her so she'll know the police are involved. Most likely, she'll want to give you a hug."

He grinned. "I can handle that."

I glanced at the clock on the wall—11:23 p.m. "It's late. I have a lot of snooping to do tomorrow."

Tucker grinned, creased his brow, and said, "Then let's get started." He took my hand and led me into the bedroom.

Chapter 9

After Tucker left the next morning, I drank another cup of coffee as I planned my day. The first thing I wanted to do was recover the bug from Georgina's blazer before she discovered it, assuming she hadn't already. Using a special program Grover provided to all of his employees, it didn't take me long to find Georgina Levin's address.

Twenty minutes later, I drove down a tree-lined street in an upper-class neighborhood and stopped two houses from Georgina's, a two-story, red brick with an immaculately manicured front yard. I checked my watch—9:40 a.m.—and figured her children would be in school at that hour. To make sure Georgina was at work, I placed a call to the hospital and asked for the administration department

"May I help you," Georgina said sweetly, and then I hung up. There was a chance my name might have appeared on her phone, but it was unlikely that seeing

Dora would raise any flags.

I got out of the car, went to her front door, and rang the doorbell as an added precaution to verify no one was inside. While I waited, I noticed an ADT sign in the flower bed that abutted the house. Making a mental note of that, I rang the bell again. Satisfied, I glanced around the neighborhood while walking away from her house. Not seeing anyone outside or peering out any windows, I doubled back and headed toward her back yard. The side gate squeaked loudly when I opened it, but it didn't appear to draw any attention. I strode to her back door and looked through its window. A steady red light shined from an alarm system on the wall about four feet from the door.

After slipping on a pair of latex gloves, I pulled out my picks. Within a minute, I was inside and working on disarming the buzzing alarm system. Once that was taken care of, I kept my head down as I searched for their modem. It sat on a table below a television hanging on the wall. I unplugged it, knowing if there were security cameras in the house, they no longer could transmit. Still, I raised my head and looked around for cameras. Not seeing any on the main floor, I headed upstairs and continued scanning for them.

The bedroom next to the stairwell had pink walls and posters of rock bands plastered everywhere— definitely the territory of a teenage girl. The adjacent bedroom had a boy's clothing tossed on top of a chair in the corner. A few soccer trophies sat on a shelf above a computer. The third bedroom looked clean and unused. I guessed it was a guest bedroom. Double doors led to the fourth bedroom. That room was appreciably larger than the other bedrooms, and it had a large ensuite bathroom with a Jacuzzi. Makeup was spread out on the counter. The door to the walk-in closet stood wide open. Only Georgina's clothing hung in the closet. Nothing in it indicated the closet was shared with a man. Since her husband had taken all of his stuff when he left or she had boxed it up, it appeared their separation was permanent.

Georgina's clothing was nicely organized—skirts, slacks, blazers, dresses, and evening attire. Her shoes and shoe boxes were neatly arranged on a bank of shelves. Spotting the blazer she had worn yesterday, I stepped toward it and pulled my bug out of the pocket.

Next, I began searching her drawers, looking for anything that might relate to that night. Then I thought about the way Sheila swayed before she was struck by a car and went back into the bathroom to check the medicine cabinet. Several prescription pill containers sat on the top shelf. One was Simvastatin prescribed for her husband. The other two contained pills but no labels. I snatched one pill out of each bottle and pushed them into the front compartment of my backpack. On the shelf below that was a box that held hypodermic needles. Antiseptic and bandages were on the bottom shelf.

After rummaging through the vanity drawers, I went to the small refrigerator sitting in the corner of the bathroom. It contained a supply of bottled water, white wine, and a plastic container. I opened it and saw vials of insulin. Georgina or her husband must be a diabetic. Then I stepped back into the bedroom to continue my search. The nightstand farthest away from the bathroom only had a lamp on it. The other one was cluttered with a small notepad, pen, e-reader, an empty glass, and a clock. Assuming that was the nightstand Georgina used, I picked up the notepad. The top page was blank, but several had been torn out of it. I pulled a pencil out of my backpack and ran the edge of the lead over the notepad and picked up the words "dentist appoint." Nothing else. A journal was in the drawer. I opened it and breezed over the dated first entry. It read like a diary. Even though it held personal thoughts, I had a case to solve and to me that meant nothing was off limits.

I thumbed through it and stopped on August 18th, three days before April filed a missing person's report. Georgina's entry just summarized her day. Nothing unusual. August 19th was more interesting. That day she mentioned Jared would be going to the cabin to celebrate April's birthday and it had been four days since she last saw him. On August 20th, she wrote about seeing him in the cafeteria and how she could hardly wait for the weekend. I wondered how she planned to spend time with Jared since her husband and Colleen were going to be there. Maybe she was content just to be in his company.

As I continued reading, I learned that April's birthday was August 24th. I looked at my cell phone calendar and saw that was a Saturday. April had filed the missing person's report on a Wednesday. Assuming everyone arrived for the weekend on Friday that meant April reported Mark missing two days before she left for the cabin. I had thought Mark had met his demise at the cabin. Maybe I was on the wrong track. Then I recalled April saying on the phone that *he* didn't always carry his wallet. She had to be referring to someone she knew well in order to know that detail. If whatever happened didn't involve Mark, then who was he? And what about the car? Had April lent it to someone else to drive?

I flipped to the next page and stared at the date written on the top—August 27th. I turned back a page to August 22nd. Five days were missing. I held up the journal and inspected the seam between those entries. Some pages had been torn out. I read over her August 27th entry. "Malcolm left today. He blames me for his actions but won't talk about it."

His actions? I sank down on the bed and replayed the conversations I had overheard in my head. Jared and Georgina had talked about a "she." Georgina wondered if they were in danger from "her". Jared asked if Malcolm knew about Sheila, but they never talked like he had committed a crime. It was more like he was having a hard time dealing with whatever had gone on. And if Malcolm was the culprit, would Jared risk his livelihood to keep Malcolm safe?

A door opening snapped me out of my speculations. I put the journal back into the nightstand drawer and crept toward the hallway.

Hearing the sound of high heels clicking on the wood stairs, I quietly moved into the closet as I worried that Georgina had taken off work. The clicking noise kept getting louder. I slipped behind some of her hanging clothing, guessing any second she'd be entering the bedroom. Letting the material drape around my face, I peered out between the slats in the louvered closet door and saw a woman's back. She was too thin to be Georgina. As she turned slightly, I recognized her—April. *Why is she here?* On the phone, she'd said that she had the day off. I doubted that April knew how to pick a lock, so she must have a key. Did Georgina call her to pick something up?

I watched as April knelt down next to Georgina's dresser, pulling open and lifting out the bottom drawer. She reached into her purse, took something out, and placed it in the dresser. From my vantage point, I couldn't see what it was. Then April picked up the drawer and forced it back in place, hiding whatever she had put in the space below it.

April rose to her feet, brushed off her slacks, and looked around the room. Then her heels clicked on the floor and down the stairs. The sound of a door opening and closing reverberated through the house.

Curious what April had left behind, I left the closet, went to the dresser, and removed the bottom drawer. On the floor sat a striped sack. I opened it up and saw a plastic bag inside that held a white powder. I guessed it was either cocaine or heroin. Wanting to verify that and not having anything on me that would serve to collect a sample, I put the sack back and replaced the drawer. Keeping my ears on high alert, I cautiously moved down the stairs and went into the kitchen. Then I quickly searched the drawers, found a box of sandwich bags, and took one. Returning to Georgina's bedroom, I removed the bottom dresser drawer again and pulled out the sack. I opened the plastic bag in it, scooped up a small sample of the powder into the sandwich bag, and stuck that bag in my backpack.

Putting everything back the way April had left it, a question popped into my head. Had Georgina told April to put the sack under the dresser, a place her children wouldn't accidentally run into it? I pressed my lips together. *That doesn't make sense.* April had said on the phone to Colleen something like "I know exactly where I'm going to stash it." That didn't sound like Georgina had given her permission to hide it in her house. Maybe Detective Lindgren had really rattled April when he called the prior day. Did he say something that led her to believe she might be a suspect in the disappearance of her estranged husband? But when April initially reported him missing, the police made some calls to his parents and employer and concluded Mark Holbrook wasn't missing. He had taken a trip. No investigation was started. *Now that's changed. Mark Holbrook is officially missing and a thorough investigation has been launched.*

Not finding anything interesting or unusual in the dresser drawers, I went into the closet to check out the shoe boxes. I had only looked in a couple of them when I heard the front door open again. Had April returned?

"Mom," a teenage girl yelled. "You never set the alarm."

"Of course I did," Georgina said. "What..." her voice trailed off.

I had thought I could spend hours in Georgina's house without being disturbed. Then April showed up and now the family. I sneaked into the hallway and began moving toward the guest bedroom.

Feet pounded on the stairs and a teenager said, "Maybe Dad's been here, but why did he unplug the wifi? I'm calling him."

I immediately changed course and headed back into Georgina's closet, leaving the door ajar.

Shuffling footsteps and mumbled voices drifted through the upstairs hallway.

"It wasn't him," the teenager yelled as footfalls

bounced on the stairs. "He thinks we should call the police."

"No," Georgina said firmly. "I'm going to check the house and then we need to get going for your dentist appointment."

Hearing footfalls on the stairwell again, I ducked behind her clothing again and controlled my breathing.

"Jared, she's been at my house," Georgina said in an anxious tone. "Call me when you get this message."

Assuming the "she" was April, I figured April knew the code to turn off Georgina's alarm system since that had caused Georgina to suspect she had been there. Even if April had not shown up, Georgina still would've blamed her for turning off the alarm. But to cover her tracks, April probably would've reset it had the alarm been on when she arrived.

The closet door suddenly flew open. "April, are you hiding in here?"

As Georgina stepped into the closet, I bit my lower lip and pressed my back against the wall. The hanging clothing near me swayed liked she had brushed them with her hand.

"Mom," the teenager yelled. "I've brushed my teeth. We need to go."

"I'll be right there," Georgina shouted.

The closet door slammed shut, throwing me into pitch darkness. I continued controlling my breathing and didn't budge for at least fifteen minutes, and then I slowly inched out of the closet. Only hearing the humming sound of the small fridge in the bathroom, I made my way to the bedroom door, peered into the hallway, and intensely listened. I didn't detect any movement or voices.

Doubting they would have left without setting the alarm, I recalled the motion detector downstairs and knew the alarm would go off as soon as I went down there. I checked all the windows on the second floor. None of the windows had any wires, indicating an alarm signal would blare if they were opened, but they all had screens. That left me with two options—either remove a screen and drop it to the ground or charge through the house and unlock the backdoor while the alarm buzzed. With the latter, Georgina would know that someone had been in her house when she was there and might decide to have more security equipment installed—like cameras outside. Since there was a possibility I might want to make a return visit, I decided to go with the former.

Georgina's bedroom was at the back of the house. I looked out her bedroom windows to determine which one would be the best to climb out of. Seeing a tree near one of them, I picked that window as my escape route. A large branch extended almost to the house. It would be an easy leap to reach it. I opened the window, removed the screen, and put it under the bed in the guest bedroom. It might be a while before Georgina noticed it there. Maybe never if she had a house cleaner.

Before venturing out, I wanted to take another look at her journal. I pulled it out of her nightstand and flipped to the day before Sheila had staggered out of the hospital—September 21st. Georgina wrote about talking to Jared, almost documenting his every word. Then I turned to the next page to see what she had written on Friday, the day Sheila died. The date on it was September 23rd, not September 22nd. Like her prior entry, she had scribbled down almost everything Jared said to her on that day, including the meeting in the hallway. My eyes fixed on her last sentence—"Jared thinks April is responsible for Sheila." That confirms April was the "she" they talked about on Saturday night. Between the September 21st and September 23rd entries, there was a remnant of the page that had been torn out. It appeared Georgina had sanitized her journal, removing anything where she might have written about what happened at the cabin and Sheila's death. But, then why didn't she tear out her conversation with Jared?

I again read over what she wrote about her meeting with Jared. It inferred a crime had been committed and she played a role in it. I would have definitely torn it out. But from what I had read so far in her journal, she was crazy about Jared. Maybe that was it. She couldn't bear wiping out their personal conversation, like she held it sacred. Something she could read often.

It had been close to an hour since Georgina and her daughter left for the dentist. *They might be back soon.* Even though I wanted to spend more time reading through her journal, looking for clues that might have a bearing on Sheila's death, I felt I had already overstayed my unwelcome visit.

After putting away the journal, I smoothed the quilt on the bed to remove the indentation where I had been sitting and then positioned myself on the outside ledge, partially closed the window behind me, and leapt to the branch. Clasping my arms around it, I moved to the tree trunk and edged to a lower branch. I glanced around and saw a little three-or four-year-old girl, her brown hair in pigtails, waving at me from the neighboring yard. Not wanting her to think that I was a burglar, I smiled and waved back. Then I clambered down to the ground.

As I walked along the sidewalk toward my car, a gate squeaked open. I picked up my pace.

"Wait," a child's voice behind me yelled.

Looking over my shoulder, I saw the little brunette running toward me.

"You playin' hide an' seek?" She asked as her eyes lit up.

"The game just finished."

"Oh." Disappointment flashed on her face. "I wanna play."

"Can't today. I need to go home now."

"Get me next time." She pointed toward her house. "Live there."

"Maci!" a woman shouted.

The little girl's index finger flew to her mouth. "Shhh. Mommy say, 'Maci'..." She stamped a foot on the sidewalk "...don't leave backyard." She bounced to the side of her house, turned and waved to me.

As I waved back, her front door opened.

"Maci, are you out here?" a woman said, stepping onto the front porch.

Maci was nowhere in sight as I turned and continued to my car.

I headed to the nearest shopping center, parked and made notes about my visit to Georgina's house, and then mulled over the cabin again. April reported Mark Holbrook missing before her birthday, but I sensed he was involved in that weekend at the cabin. Maybe he drove the red Corvette and unexpectedly showed up. Maybe he was still there.

Chapter 10

I drove to the hospital to get Sheila's medical records. With the inaccurate toxicology report placed in her record that showed no drugs in her system, Jared had told Georgina there was no reason not to release it. I doubted there would be anything in her record that would shed any light on my investigation, but I wanted a copy.

Within twenty minutes, the technician in the records department handed me a copy of Sheila Wilson's hospital medical records. I stuck them in my backpack and went to Jared's office in the adjacent medical building. Strolling through his office door, I overheard the woman behind the counter telling a man that Dr. Ebert would be in surgery all day. *Can't plant a bug on him today.*

Since Georgina sounded anxious to talk to Jared, and thinking they might meet someplace again for that conversation, I retrieved a long range bug from my backpack. Gripping it in my hand, I walked into the administration department. Unlike Saturday, every desk in there was occupied.

The minute Georgina looked up, her eyes locked on me. She stood and headed toward me. "Were you able to obtain the medical records you wanted?"

Seeing she was wearing a sweater with pockets over a nicely tailored blue dress, I smiled to myself. "Yes. I just came to thank you for trying to help me on Saturday." As her eyes narrowed, I skillfully lowered the bug and slipped it into her pocket.

"You're welcome," she said hesitantly.

"Well, thanks again, and I'll let you know if I need anything else."

She tilted her head and pressed her lips together.

I swirled around and walked out of the administration department. There was no doubt in my mind that Georgina believed I was up to something. Since this case didn't require me to go undercover, I hoped she had assumed I was an investigator. That information puts people who have something to hide on edge and often talk to a confidant about it. And with the bug in her pocket, I wanted her talking.

I hurried to my car, climbed in, and flipped on my listening device.

"...following me," Georgina's voice came through the speaker. "Yes. 7:30."

Only soft garbled voices came next. I guessed she had been talking on the phone and hung up. I glanced at my watch—3:20 p.m.

Without turning off the listening device, I placed a call to Tucker. His cell went right to voicemail. "Hey, I've acquired some white substance. Since it involves the cabin, would you like me to bring it there to have it tested or take it to the lab Grover uses?" I disconnected, adjusted the listening device to record only, and called Maddie.

"Oh, thank you, thank you, Dora," she said the minute she answered. "The police have picked up Sheila's body to test for drugs. When Tucker called, he didn't say you were behind it, but I just knew you were. How did you convince him?"

"Well, you know, I *do* know how to please him."

"Yeah, right. He wouldn't be swayed that way. He'd want some kind of evidence that the hospital report was wrong."

"I really shouldn't tell you my investigative secrets."

"Come on, Dora, share."

"I collected a tube of Sheila's blood in the hospital. It showed positive for drugs, but I couldn't prove it came from Sheila. That's why they needed her body."

"That makes sense. You could've taken that blood from any druggie that strolled into the hospital, and there are plenty of those."

"You know, I hadn't even thought about that. It probably would've been a lot simpler than sneaking into the morgue and snatching it."

"See. I know how to help you out on your investigations. Hey, the form I signed to release Sheila's body to the medical examiner also gave permission to perform an autopsy if needed. Why would that be necessary?"

"Maddie, I have no idea. Your guess would be better than mine."

"It has me stymied. All I've been able to come up with is if they are trying to determine cause of death. From everything I know, she actually died from being hit by a car. Do you think they're questioning that?"

I shrugged. "I doubt it. They probably had you sign a standard form that included that contingency, but, Maddie, don't mention to your co-workers or anyone associated with the hospital that the medical examiner has taken possession of Sheila's body."

"Understood."

"Good. You're sounding better today. How are you feeling?"

"Better. I've taken bereavement leave. That gives me another week off. Tobias is staying with me. He thinks I should stay at his place. You know… so I wouldn't feel the constant void of Sheila not being here, but staying at his place would just delay the inevitable. You getting closer to finding her killer?"

"I'm following up on some leads."

"Anything you can tell me about?"

"Not yet," I said, thinking I could be barking up the wrong tree, and I didn't want to get Maddie's hopes up. "I need to get back to it. I'll call when I have something concrete. Say hi to Tobias for me."

"When Sheila's murderer is behind bars, I might even decide to marry him."

"Well, you couldn't go wrong with Tobias. He loves you."

"I know."

After we said goodbye, I listened to what had been recorded on the machine while I spoke with Maddie. Only business. Nothing interesting. I left it on while I opened the envelope that contained Sheila's medical records. My eyes popped wide open when I saw the name of her emergency room doctor—April Holbrook. As I continued scanning over the report, my cell rang.

"Hi, Tee," I answered, pushing the listening device's record button.

"April Holbrook's interview just ended. You at home?"

"No."

"You able to meet me there?"

"Yes. See you in a few." I hung up and put the medical records back into the envelope.

As I drove home, I wondered what Tucker had learned in the interview that caused him to want to tell me about it right away—something he couldn't do at the precinct. I also had info I wanted to share with him.

I pulled into the driveway and stopped next to Tucker's unmarked police car.

Entering the house, I heard Tucker in the kitchen. Papers were spread all over the kitchen table. "Looks like you've been busy."

"You might say that. You want one?" he asked, holding up a can of beer.

"Yeah."

When we were both settled at the table, Tucker began. "Stan was surprised how nervous Holbrook was today. He had spoken with her often—a couple of times at the hospital. She was always calm on those occasions. Not today. She twisted and played with her bracelet during the entire interview."

"Did she bring a lawyer with her?"

"No, but the interview stopped when she refused to answer any more questions without her lawyer present."

"So she's lawyered up."

"If she hasn't retained a lawyer yet to deal with the matter, she'll be busy getting one."

"What did you find out?"

"Earlier today, Stan talked to Hank Powers, the owner of the convenience store close to Feister's cabin, and asked about Mark Holbrook. Powers remembered seeing him a few days before a woman named Betsy Fogel complained about gun shots coming from the Feister property. Powers serves on the local council. He looked up the date he put a notice on their gate—August 27th. He thought that was a day or two after Betsy had complained to him.

"When Stan asked April Holbrook if her husband might be staying at the cabin, she stammered for an answer. She finally said that she had gone there for her birthday and hadn't been back since, so she didn't know.

"Stan asked her numerous questions about her last visit to the cabin. Her answers coincided with what Maddie had told you—Her birthday was August 24th. Her sister, Colleen, and Colleen's husband, Jared Ebert, and her cousin, Georgina, and Georgina's husband, Malcolm Levin, were also at the cabin, helping her celebrate. They all arrived on Friday and left on Sunday. Then Stan asked if guns were kept at the cabin for hunting. She acted indignant that he would even ask that, like she was an anti-gun person, and claimed that no one in her family even owned a gun and certainly no one hunted. Stan decided to press the point and told her that a neighbor had complained about hearing gunshots coming from the Feister property. Holbrook demanded to know where he had heard that. He calmly said a confidential source. She went on and said that the neighbor had to be mistaken. If guns were fired in that area, which wasn't allowed, the shooter couldn't possibly be anyone staying at the cabin.

"Then Stan mentioned that her husband had been seen in the area around her birthday. If he wasn't staying at the cabin, did he have friends in the area? That was when April didn't want to answer any more questions without a lawyer present."

"I'm surprised she showed up at the precinct without one. Something went down at the cabin the weekend of her birthday. Something unlawful."

"She didn't know anything was going to be discussed about the cabin."

"April had to at least suspect that might be brought up. Otherwise, why did she hurry and go there to collect that sack and check the grounds after Stan called to ask her to come to the police station?"

"Some people believe if they show up with an attorney, it makes them look guilty. She might be one of those."

"Did Hank Powers by any chance mention what type of car Mark Holbrook was driving when he saw him?"

"I had Stan ask him that question. According to Powers, Mark didn't have a car. He had walked to the store. Let me see that powder sample."

I took the sandwich bag out of my backpack.

Tucker opened it, tapped his index finger on his tongue, and stuck it in the bag. Next, he put the powder coated finger in his mouth and tasted the substance. "Cocaine. High quality."

I tilted my head and squinted. "How much experience have you had with that type of stuff?"

"Enough. Where did you get this?"

"While I was visiting Georgina's house..."

"Visiting? You mean you broke in?"

"Let's just say I was an unwelcome guest. April Holbrook showed up. She was also an unwelcome guest. She hid a sack, which looks exactly like the one she got at the cabin, under Georgina's dresser."

"April might have discussed it with Georgina, and Georgina suggested that would be a good place to hide it."

I squinted. "Do you actually believe that?"

"No, but that possibility does exist."

"Well, that wasn't the case. When Georgina came home to take her daughter to the dentist, the alarm wasn't on. She called someone and said in a very unpleased tone 'she' had been there."

"Who was Georgina talking to?"

I shrugged. "Someone's voicemail. Georgina told that person to call her. My guess would be Jared. She's meeting someone today at 7:30. I don't know where."

"Any way you could find out?"

I lifted the listening device out of my bag. "Maybe she'll mention it."

"You bugged her again?"

"Yep. Right now, it's recording. Since she's at work, the bug picks up a lot of meaningless chatter. I'll play the recording in a little while." She looked up. "Oh, I talked to Maddie, and she was wondering why the medical examiner might do an autopsy."

"So far, drugs have been found in the blood. He had other concerns and intends to perform an autopsy."

"Maddie thought the only reason an autopsy would be necessary was if the medical examiner questioned the cause of death. Is that it?"

"I'll know more tomorrow. Do you plan to follow

Georgina Levin to this evening's meeting?"

"Yes. I want to know if April follows her. A gray Volvo followed Georgina last time she met Jared, and that's the type of car April drives." Then I glanced at my watch—5:10 p.m. Too late to call my DMV contact. "Hey, can you get me April Holbrook's license plate number?"

"Yes, if I can tag along with you tonight."

"But you don't approve of my methods."

"True. Since Mark Holbrook is still missing and gunshots were heard around the same time he was seen in the cabin area, Stan will be obtaining a warrant to search the cabin and surrounding grounds. He should have it tomorrow. Even if something is discovered that might lead to the missing Mark Holbrook..."

I interrupted. "Like his body?"

Tucker slightly nodded. "That won't tell us who committed the crime. Whatever we overhear Levin saying won't be admissible evidence. Still, it might be useful in locating some admissible evidence. If anything is said that connects Sheila to whatever went down at the cabin, it could bring us a step closer to determining why she was drugged."

"I mentioned earlier that Jared thinks Sheila's death was because he told her about the incident at the cabin. He thought 'she' was responsible for drugging Sheila. And *she* is April, but I lack anything that would substantiate his assumption."

"Dee, the night you overheard that, you weren't recording the conversation. So you have nothing." He leaned over and tapped my temple. "What's in there doesn't count."

Cocking my head, I said, "That's why I won't stop

bugging Georgina until the case is solved. And she's not the only one I intend to keep track off."

"What time should we leave?" Tucker asked as if I had given him permission to tag along.

"Six-fifteen. I'll check for the location of the bug before we leave to determine if she's at home or at the hospital."

"Let me make a call." He stood and went into the den without picking up any of the documents on the table.

Staring at them, I couldn't resist the urge to glance through the papers. While I read Stan Lindgren's summation of his call with Hank, Tucker strode into the kitchen, startling me.

"Find anything new?"

"No. Since you left all of these on the table, didn't that mean it was okay for me to look at them?"

"It did," he said, surprising me. "But there isn't anything in there I haven't already summarized for you."

"Seeing the toxicology report reminded me that I had forgotten to give you these." I pulled the unidentified pills out of my pocket and handed them to Tucker. "In Georgina's medicine cabinet, there were two unlabeled pill containers. Those pills came from them. Do you want to handle having them analyzed, or should I do that?"

Tucker examined them. "Why don't you take care of it? I don't want to explain how they came into my possession." He gave the pills back to me.

"I'll do that in the morning."

"This is the license plate number of April Holbrook's gray Volvo." He placed a note on the table.

I took my notepad out of my backpack and found the page that contained the four digits of the Volvo that had followed Georgina to the bar and then followed Jared when he left. Comparing them to the digits in Tucker's note, I said, "The first four are a perfect match to those I wrote down. It appears April followed them. Assuming Georgina is going to meet Jared, let's see if she does a repeat performance tonight."

After skimming through a few more of Tucker's documents, I went into the den and played the recording on my listening device while Tucker packed snacks to take with us on the surveillance. Mumbled voices came through the device. Georgina chatted with another woman about work as high heels clicked on a hard surface.

Georgina's last words to the woman were "See you tomorrow." A few minutes later, she said, "I have to work late tonight….Yes, order pizza. There's money in the usual place…When it gets dark, set the alarm…Yes, on stay… Call me if there's a problem…Love you. Bye."

I sighed with relief since I had been concerned that Georgina might change her clothes if she went home after work which probably would mean the bugged sweater wouldn't be going with her to the 7:30 appointment. I glanced at my watch—6:08 p.m. To verify Georgina was still at the hospital, I tapped into the location of the bug. It showed the address of Feister Northwest Hospital.

After stuffing a few supplies in my backpack, I left the den for my first stakeout with Tucker.

Chapter 11

Pulling into the hospital's parking lot, I spotted a blue Lexus and slowly drove by it, checking the license plate number. "That's Georgina's car," I said.

"Is that Jared Ebert's white Porsche?" Tucker pointed at a vehicle in the petitioned off parking section for doctors.

"I don't have his license plate number, but there is a bug inside his car." I swung into a slot on the next row where we had a clear view of both vehicles. Turning off the engine, I said, "I'll check if it's his." I reached into the back seat and grabbed my listening device and found the location. "His car is here someplace. If that's not it, then there's another white Porsche in the parking lot. It's probably easier for Jared to stay at the hospital if he's going to be meeting with Georgina than to tell his wife another lie why he wouldn't be staying home." Leaving the device on record, I flipped a switch so we could also hear everything Georgina said.

As murmured voices came through the device, Tucker asked, "Did you notice a gray Volvo parked in front of the medical building next to the hospital?"

I shook my head. "No. Where you able to catch the license number?"

"We didn't drive by it. I saw it when you turned the corner."

"Interesting." Assuming it was April's car, I wondered how she learned about the meeting. Did she talk often to her sister? Could Colleen have mentioned Jared was working late? From what I heard when Jared met Georgina at Tilly's, he thought "she" would want to know who told Sheila. If April knew or suspected her brother-in-law was having an affair with Sheila, she had to surmise that Jared was the one who squealed. Maybe she was following him to confirm her suspicion. I gestured toward a man walking in the parking lot. "That's Jared."

Tucker and I both stared out the front windshield as he went into the fenced off doctors' section, climbed into the white Porsche, and drove away.

I tapped on the steering wheel. "Too bad we can't see the Volvo from here."

"If the Volvo belongs to April Holbrook and Georgina Levin is meeting Ebert, we might see it later." Tucker pulled two snack bars out of a bag and handed me one. Between bites, he said, "It's almost seven. Georgina's meeting spot must be close to here."

"Tilly's, the place she met Jared on Saturday night, is about a twenty-five-minute drive," I said while the sound of a door shutting came through the speaker followed by a clicking noise.

"Sounds like she's on the move."

Within five minutes, I started the engine, left the parking lot, and drove a few cars behind the Lexus.

"There's a gray Volvo in the far right lane," Tucker said, covering part of his face with his hand. "Move to the center lane, and I'll check the license plate number."

My eyes darted between the Lexus and the cars in the abutting lane. At my first opportunity, I cut into that lane, a half a car length behind and to the left of the Volvo. I slightly slowed down so Tucker could catch the number.

Keeping his face partially hidden, he said, "It's April Holbrook's car. She knows who I am."

"Do you think she has already seen you?"

"I doubt she's on the lookout for someone else to be on Levin's tail. She's focused on keeping track of the Lexus. Most likely, other cars wouldn't even register with her unless she saw red-and-blue flashing lights."

"They'd register with me too, but since I have a cop sitting by my side, I'm not too worried about it."

"Don't have that type of…"

"Duck down or cover your face with something."

"Why?" Tucker picked up my notepad and held it next to his face.

"The Volvo driver. Her hair. When I saw April, her hair was appreciably longer than the driver's. I guess she could've had it cut since Sunday, but I want to check."

Tucker leaned back in the seat, keeping the notepad in front of his face while I drove a little faster to see the driver. Then suddenly, I noticed Georgina signaling to move into the far left lane.

"I can't check now." I flipped on my left blinker. "It looks like Georgina might be planning to make a left turn. If that's the case, she's not going to Tilly's."

With the heavy traffic and no one slowing down to let me into that lane, I watched Georgina move into the left turn lane as I went straight through the intersection. "Georgina's turning. We're going to have to double back." Then I glanced to my right, looking for the Volvo. "I don't see the Volvo anywhere."

Tucker sat straight up and glanced around. "Maybe the driver turned right at that intersection and, like us, is doubling back in search of Georgina."

"Possibly." I made a U-ey at the next intersection and then turned right onto the street that Georgina had taken and drove for several blocks, not seeing a blue Lexus anywhere. "So much for my tailing abilities." I cut to the curb.

"It's my fault for having you move into another lane."

"Yep, it sure is." I looked at Tucker and grinned. "I guess I'm going to have to think twice about taking you with me on another stakeout."

"Don't be so hard on yourself." He gave me that sensuous smile that I loved. "Think about what you'd be missing." He leaned closer, wrapped his arms around me, and planted a passionate kiss on my lips, a kiss that sent a tingling sensation through my body.

"Is that how you treat all of your partners on the way to a stakeout?"

"Yes. I try to treat everyone equally."

I playfully slugged his shoulder.

"Ouch," he moaned and grabbed his shoulder. "Didn't know you could throw such a power punch."

"Right. Do you want me to stop someplace so you

can get a cold pack for your injured shoulder?"

A hint of a smile crossed his lips as he moved his shoulder in circles. "Let's see if it heals on its own."

"Now, time to get back to work." Since only music came through the device's speaker, I figured Georgina hadn't reached her destination yet. I checked the gadget for the bug's location and tapped it into my GPS.

"She turned right at the intersection we just passed." I edged back into the traffic.

While I made the necessary turns to get on the same road that Georgina was traveling, Tucker pulled out his cell. "I'm going to get Ebert's license plate number."

About ten minutes later, the music stopped, and Georgina's voice came through the device. "Jared, I don't want you to get the wrong impression because we've been here before, but I couldn't think of another place where we could talk privately."

"No problem. Have you discovered…"

"Let's talk when we get inside."

The pounding of feet going up stairs echoed through the car, followed by a soft, clicking noise.

"They're unlocking a door," Tucker commented as a door opened and closed.

Then shuffling of feet and squeaking sounds drifted through the speaker. A few minutes later, Georgina gasped and moaned. "Oh, Jared."

Tucker and I exchanged a look.

Sarcastically, I said, "Sounds like he's really missing Sheila."

"From what you told me, the boy gets around."

Besides moans, groans, and heavy breathing, nothing else came over the listening device as I slowed down near a motel, the place where the bug was located.

"Georgina has the hots for Jared," I said. "She wants more than just to talk about a problem; otherwise, she never would have picked a motel."

"And they've been there before."

As I started to pull into the parking lot, Tucker grabbed my notepad and held it up, shielding his face. "There's a gray Volvo parked in the back row, facing the motel. Driver's still inside."

I drove by the Volvo to check the license plate number and to take a quick look at the driver. "It's April's car, but I doubt the driver is her." I stopped in a spot at the end of the row.

Tucker tilted his head and rubbed his chin. "Who do you think it might be?"

"I'd guess Colleen."

"We can't remain in the car. It'll draw the driver's attention. She's going to be expecting us to check it. Neither April nor Colleen have seen you. Go and get us a room."

That was exactly what I had planned to suggest. I climbed out of the car and headed to the office, trying to get a better look at the driver on my way. She was leaning against the steering wheel, so I couldn't be positive she was the same woman in the Twitter post, but I was certain that she wasn't the thin April.

I managed to get us a room on the second floor, not so we'd be close to Jared and Georgina, but so we could keep track of the gray Volvo and the driver inside. As I slid back into the car, I asked, "Are Jared and Georgina talking or still just making sounds?"

"Just sounds, and it sounds like they're having a good time," Tucker said with a wide smile. "I seldom go on a stake out and get that type of entertainment."

"Then you need to go with me more often. Those noises are quite common. In case the woman I saw at the cabin and in Georgina's house isn't April, can you describe her?"

"Thin, 5 foot 7, oval face, green eyes, long medium-brown hair—it was in a ponytail when she came to the station. Even though she's thin, April has a firm body, like she could be a runner."

"The woman in the Volvo is definitely not April." I held up the keys. "Room 214."

We gathered up all our stuff and headed to the room. Before we got settled, Jared's voice blared through the speaker. "You want to go first?"

"Yes. Just give me a minute."

A door opened and closed.

While I positioned my notepad and the listening device on the table, Tucker spread out some snacks and sodas on it. "Thanks," I said, tearing open a candy bar."

"Did you figure out why April dropped by your house?" Jared asked.

"I haven't had a chance to look around, but she wasn't the person who drugged Sheila before the accident."

"What makes you believe April didn't slip Sheila something? After all, she's the one that has the most to lose if anyone talks."

"I checked April's schedule. All afternoon she was busy dealing with back-to-back emergency room patients. Seven came in from an industrial accident about three hours before Sheila's accident. April wouldn't have had any time to hunt down Sheila and drug her. She never left the ER. One of the nurses in the ER is a good friend. She told me how April rushed to Sheila the minute she was wheeled in. April took care of Sheila before she was taken up to surgery, and April cried when she heard Sheila had died. Jared, it wasn't her."

"The blood tests were switched. It had to be someone at the hospital. April, you, and I are the only ones who work there."

"Colleen was at the hospital that day. We had lunch together. Do you think it could be her?"

"I hadn't even thought about her."

"Jared, that's the problem. You seldom think about her."

"Colleen and I are married in name only. You know that."

"And I also know that's not what she wants."

No one spoke for a few minutes. Then Jared said, "Colleen is close to her sister. Sheila and April hung out together all the time. I can envision Sheila saying something to April about the cabin incident—maybe to reassure her that she'd keep the secret safe. Sheila and Colleen didn't know each other well enough to have a personal conversation."

"Did April know about you and Sheila?"

"No. Sheila swore she'd never tell her."

"If she mentioned the cabin to April, April would ask her how she knows about it."

"Good point. Over the years, Sheila has made a few enemies at the hospital. I had just assumed her death was somehow related to what had occurred at the cabin."

"Jared, did you tell her?...It's okay. I won't blame you if did. You and Sheila had a very special relationship."

"Sheila thought I might be involved with another woman since I seemed uptight when we were together. She would have left me had I not told her what was bothering me, but she would have kept it a secret."

"Then why do you think she might have mentioned it to April or anyone?"

"I don't know," Jared said, his voice dragging. "She died a few days after I told her. That's probably why."

"Maybe you should just let it go."

"Stop trying to find out who's guilty? I can't do that. I need answers. I need to know if I'm responsible."

"The tox report was clean. The police aren't going to be looking for anyone."

"But they are. Colleen told me that April was questioned about Mark's disappearance, and the detective mentioned Mark had been seen in that area near the cabin. Others could be questioned. If anything comes out about my relationship with Sheila that might lead the police into looking further into her death."

"What...what did April say?"

"Even if Mark was around there, he never went to the cabin."

"Anything else?"

"Something about April was going to bring a lawyer if the detective wanted to talk to her again."

"That doesn't sound good."

"I suspect old man Feister will make it all go away," Jared said in a disgusted tone.

"You really think so?"

"Look at all the DUI's and illegal drug possessions

he got wiped off of April's record."

"A missing husband is quite a few steps above that. Should we all lawyer up?"

"No…no…be cool if you're questioned. Remember none of us saw Mark that weekend."

"Let me know if they question you."

"I will."

"I have to get going. The kids believe I'm working late, but showing up much past ten might be hard to explain. If you can't let Sheila's death go, I wouldn't rule out Colleen, but I don't know if you want to go down that road. What if you found out it was her? What would you do?"

"Georgina, I don't know…. I could never turn in the mother of my son."

"Well, think about it."

"Thanks, Georgina. I don't know what I would do if I couldn't confide in you."

"And I feel the same way."

A door opened.

I peered out the edge of the drapes, looking for Georgina. She didn't walk past the window. I spotted her when she stepped into the parking lot. As she drove away, my eyes darted to the gray Volvo. The driver still sat behind the steering wheel.

"Is she gone?" Tucker asked.

"Yes and the Volvo hasn't budged. I'd think by now, the driver would be getting pretty bored."

"Last time, I overheard Jared and Georgina talking, Georgina said 'blood tests.' Jared said the same 'blood tests' today. Besides the toxicology test, do you know if another blood test could also show if drugs results?"

Tucker shrugged. "For drugs, we request the

toxicology report. I don't know if that information would show up on another blood test report. Why?"

"Just curious. It just strikes me as odd that they've both used the word 'tests' and not 'test.' Maybe blood type and stuff like that is on all the blood tests performed on a person, so all the blood tests have to be switched to make it look legit."

Not hearing music coming through the device, I said, "I guess Georgina isn't going to be listening to the radio on her way home.

Tucker shook his head. "Listen." He pointed to the gadget while the sound of a toilet flushing came through the speaker.

"The bug is still in their room."

Tucker nodded.

"I need to know their room number," I said, walking toward the door. "I'm going to pretend I'm getting something out of the car so I can see the room Jared exists."

I hurried out the door and ran smack into Jared, leaving the next room. "Sorry," I said, skirting around him and heading to soda pop machine near the office."

Carrying a soda, I slowly went up the stairs as Jared pulled out of the parking lot and watched the headlights of the Volvo flip on.

"She's following Jared," I said, strolling into the room. "So, what's the verdict?"

"Everyone at the cabin was involved with Mark Holbrook's disappearance, but April has the most to lose if someone talks. That could infer April was responsible for Mark's disappearance."

"You mean she killed him?"

"That's up to a court to decide. Right now, we

don't have any evidence that he's even dead."

"I suspect something will show up tomorrow if Stan gets a warrant. You think Feister can squash that?"

Tucker shrugged. "Stan mentioned that April Holbrook had a clean record."

"It sounds like it was scrubbed pretty good. What about Sheila?"

"From what I heard, I'm not convinced the cabin incident had anything to do with her death."

"Same here. My first thought was one of Jared's jealous ex-lovers or his wife was responsible for the drugging. I just don't know if any of them would be in a position to switch tox reports."

"Since we know the one given to the accident investigator wasn't accurate, the hospital will be informed and their practices will be audited. During that process, the precinct will learn who has access to those reports."

"If I could get a copy of that list, I might be able to determine something.… Hey, I never heard anyone mention Feister's wife. Is Colleen's and April's mother out of the picture?"

Tucker nodded. "Stan wanted to talk to her about Mark Holbrook's disappearance and found out that she took off when Colleen and April were kids. Feister has raised the girls by himself. He often took his oldest daughter, Colleen, to social events when she was in high school and college."

"What about April?" I asked, recalling the pictures I saw of young Colleen with her father at some of those events.

"After Colleen married, he started taking her." Tucker took a sip of his soda. "Let's get out of here."

"Oh, I have to find the bug first."

Chapter 12

The following morning shortly before Tucker left for the precinct, he told me he'd let me know if Stan managed to get the search warrant. Even though I was starting to doubt that whatever had gone on at the cabin had a bearing on Sheila's death, I wasn't about to rule it out until I had all the answers.

I sat at my desk, finishing up my notes from the prior night's outing and waited for Tucker's call. I had just emptied my second cup of coffee when my cell rang.

"Stan got it. I'm going with him."

"The gate's locked. How are you planning to enter the property?"

"When Stan talked to Hank Powers, the store owner, Powers said that Feister has a cleaning lady. She's his cousin and has a key to the gate and cabin. She used to clean the place once a week, but she was told they were doing a little fix up and would call her when they were ready to have it cleaned again. Stan will inform Dr. Raymond Feister about the search when we reach the cabin."

"Good. So even if he should have high-ranking friends in the police department, he won't have time to stop the search before it's underway. Since Feister wasn't at the cabin that weekend, he might be completely in the dark as to whatever happened there."

"That's what I'm thinking, but as soon as he gets the call, he'll be contacting his daughters."

"It's time for me to plant another bug." After hanging up, I quickly dressed and then left for the hospital.

Twenty-minutes later, I walked down the hall toward the administration department. When I was about twenty feet from the door, I heard Georgina say, "I'm going to take a break. I'll be back in fifteen minutes."

I swung around and headed toward the lobby. Then I stopped and glanced over my shoulder. Georgina was walking the opposite direction. I back-tracked and hurried into the administration department. The double-door behind Georgina's desk, which I figured led to Dr. Feister's office, was ajar. As I moved toward it, a short, heavyset woman stood up from another desk and asked, "May I help you?"

"I have an appointment with Dr. Feister."

She thumbed through some documents on the top of Georgina's desk. "I don't see his appointment book. He must have it in his office. Let me tell him you're here. What is your name?"

"Sally Richards."

She walked toward his office with me right behind her. The woman turned around. "Miss Richards, please have a seat. I'll let you know when he's ready to see you."

"I'm on a tight schedule. I'll only take a few minutes of his time." I whisked by the woman and charged into Feister's office. The woman was only a couple of steps behind me.

"What's going on?" Feister asked, rising from his chair.

"Dr. Feister, I'm sorry," she said. "I asked Miss Richards to wait so I could let you know she was here."

As she spoke, I edged closer to him.

Feister's attention turned to me. "Miss Richards, I don't recall seeing your name on my appointment schedule."

"But I made it last week."

"And why did you want to see me?"

"Oh, you have such a nice view here," I said, walking around his desk to the window, but I had to admit he had a crappy view—a parking lot.

"Miss Richards, why did you want to see me?" Feister repeated in a sharp tone, his face as hard as granite.

Turning toward him, I stuck a bug in the bottom corner of the windowsill. "I'm doing a school report about hospital administration. I set up an appointment to interview you." I gave him a warm smile.

"My schedule is completely booked up today. My administrative assistant schedules all my appointments. You'll have to talk to her."

"Oh, thank you, thank you," I said, grabbing and

shaking his hand. Then I quickly left, wanting to get out of there before Georgina returned.

Sitting in my car, I checked to make sure the bug was properly functioning. No sound came through the speaker. I pressed my lips together, thinking I should have planted the bug on the man.

Then a door squeaked open.

"I understand you had a visitor while I was on break," Georgina said.

"Yes, a Sally Richards. If she calls for an appointment, I do not want to see her again," Feister said in a harsh tone.

"Understood. Was there anything else you wanted to discuss with me?"

"No. That's everything."

A door closed.

The bug works. I thought I smiled so nicely at him, and now he doesn't ever want to see me again. *How can that be?*

Guessing it would be at least another forty-five minutes before Tucker and Stan, along with the squad team, reached the cabin, I decided to swing by Eberts' house to get a better look at Colleen to verify she was the woman driving the Volvo the prior night.

* * *

After parking near Eberts' house, I retrieved a bug, a small black one that could stick to any clothing, purse, or shoes, out of my backpack. Since I didn't know who was responsible for Sheila's death, and Georgina had mentioned that Colleen was in the hospital that day, I needed more information to narrow down my prime suspects. As I climbed out of my car, a woman dressed in a yoga outfit, came out the front door and walked at a rapid pace to a dark green Mercedes in the driveway. I recognized her and approached before she got into the car, noting that Colleen's Twitter post hadn't done her justice. She was prettier and had a nice, curvy figure. Even though I couldn't clearly see the face of the woman in the Volvo the prior night, I did see enough of her features to assume it was Colleen Ebert.

"Hello, Mrs. Sorensen," I said, giving her a made-up name.

"I'm not Mrs. Sorensen," Colleen replied.

"Oh, is she inside?"

"No one lives here by that name."

I pulled out a notepad and glanced at it. "Well, the agency must have given me the wrong address. Do you have a neighbor named Sorenson?"

"Sorry. There are no Sorensons in the neighborhood." She held up her hand in a stop motion. "A family is visiting the Marshalls. Maybe that's their last name. The Marshalls live on the other side of the street." She gestured toward the house.

"Thank you," I said, sticking the bug onto the side of her black purse as she looked toward the neighbor's house. I doubted it would be easily noticed.

She slid into her car, and I headed across the street to the Marshalls. I had intended to return to my car as soon as Colleen left, but her car engine hadn't even started when I reached the house across the street. So, I rang the Marshalls' doorbell and continued with my façade of pretending to look for Mrs. Sorenson.

After I was told that no Sorensons lived there, the Mercedes still hadn't budged. With droopy shoulders,

I walked past it on the way to my car. Guessing Colleen was on her phone, I pushed a button on my listening device, the button I had set to the newly planted bug.

"….like it. Maybe you should talk to Dad," Colleen said.

"Remember what he said last time," came the voice that I recognized as belonging to April.

"But they know he was around there. You might need Dad's help and then some. You better talk to him before he gets a whiff that the police are snooping around."

"I called to tell you about it," April huffed. "Not for you to lecture me about what I should or shouldn't do."

"And how are you going to handle…the hospital problem?"

"For the umpteenth time, it wasn't me! I still think it was Georgina. Why else did she show up in the emergency room almost the second Sheila was brought in? We've seen her ogling Jared. That's why Malcolm left her."

"That wasn't a problem when she lived in another state. It's too bad they moved back here. She's been staring amorously at Jared for over two years. If that was the reason, Malcolm would have left before now."

"Next time you use my car to keep track of your hubby, return it with a full tank of gas. There wasn't even enough gas left in it for me to make it to work."

"Sorry. I'm going to be late for my class."

"And I have to get back…too many emergencies."

"Let me know if you hear anything else."

"You can count on it."

As Colleen drove away, I mulled over what I had just heard. Colleen apparently thought April played a hand in Sheila's death, and April thought Georgina was responsible. And Georgina told Jared that she thinks Colleen was behind it. I *did* learn something new—Georgina was in the emergency room at the same time Sheila was brought in. Then I recalled Sheila stopping and looking at the hospital before she continued to the street. Did she think someone was watching her?

I flipped my listening device to pick up the Feister's bug. All I heard was the sound of shuffling paper, no voices. Since that bug could transmit over a long range, I pulled away from the curb and headed out of Colleen's neighborhood. I stopped in a parking lot and made notes while I waited for Stan's call to Feister to come through the speaker.

Twenty minutes later, my cell rang and Tucker's name appeared on the screen. "Are you there?" I asked.

"Feister's cleaning lady is unlocking the gate. Stan's going to hold off placing a courtesy call to Raymond Feister until after we start our search. Are you all set?"

Tucker might not approve of my methods, but he still gave me a heads up when we shared information. "Yes. How many are there?"

"Nine counting Stan and me. We brought equipment to dig if probable cause warrants it."

"Did you get the results from Sheila's autopsy?"

"The preliminary results. The final report should be on my desk this afternoon."

"Anything new?"

"Yes, but I want to see the final report before we talk about it. The caravan has started to enter the property. If you should go into the hospital, be cautious around anyone carrying a hypodermic needle. Need to go." Tucker hung up before I could ask any questions about his warning.

Putting down my phone, I guessed that the medical examiner had determined that the drugs in Sheila's blood had been injected rather than swallowed. On that thought, I called the lab where I had dropped off the unidentified pills. The technician told me the oval white one was a calcium supplement and the round one was lorazepam, sold under the name Ativan. From dealing with other clients, I already knew that Ativan was prescribed to treat anxiety and anxiety with depression. Georgina and Jared had talked about Malcolm at the bar like he was having a hard time handling whatever went down at the cabin. Even if April thought he left Georgina because of her attraction to Jared, April could have it wrong. I also wondered how long Georgina had pined for Jared. Being Colleen's cousin, she had to have seen him often over the past twenty years. Had she always fantasized about him?

A knock snapped me out of my contemplations.

I stared at the source, my listening device, and pushed a button so it would record while I listened. In case anything was mentioned about Sheila, I didn't want to take a chance of missing it.

"I said I didn't want to be disturbed," Feister snapped.

A door squeaked open. "But Dr. Feister," said an unfamiliar female voice. "there's a police detective on the phone. He'd like to speak with you."

He sighed deeply. "Send the call through."

A peep sounded.

"This is Dr. Feister. How may I help you officer...You certainly will not!...How did you manage to obtain a search warrant?...No...don't you dare touch another thing...No, get off of my property, or I'll have your badge—Officer...Officer Lindgren...That's ridiculous..."

A banging noise came over the speaker, followed by Feister's voice. "Get Phillip on the line."

Feister told Phillip, who I guessed was his attorney, about the search, and he wanted it stopped. Then came some clicking sounds, and I assumed he was making another call. "Send April Holbrook to my office right now...Get someone else to take care of the patient...No." That was followed by more banging and clicking sounds. "Damn voicemail...Colleen, I want you in my office as soon as you can get here."

Loud pounding footsteps and wood hitting wood, which I took to be a door smacking into a wall, reverberated through the speaker. "Where's Georgina?" Feister huffed.

"On break," a woman said.

"Find her and have her report to my office."

"Yes, Dr. Feister."

As a door slammed shut again, a phone chirped. Probably his cell phone. "How long?...The police are searching the cabin and the grounds...Mark is missing... What has your sister done this time?...Colleen, it's very gallant of you to try to protect her..."

A knock on the door.

"Come in," Feister said. "Colleen, your sister and Georgina just stepped into my office. I'll put you on speaker while you're driving here." He stared at his daughter. "April, why didn't you tell me that Mark was missing?"

"I told you we were separated."

"That's a far cry from missing. Why are they searching the cabin and surrounding property?"

"Someone saw Mark around there," April said, her voice quivering. "I'm sure they're just looking for a lead to his whereabouts."

"Did he attend your birthday party there?"

"No. If he was around there during that weekend, I didn't see him."

"Georgina and Colleen, is that true?"

Everyone fell silent.

"So, it isn't true," Feister surmised. "Georgina, did something happen that weekend between April and Mark?"

"Father, I just pulled into the parking lot. I'll be in there soon," Colleen said.

"We'll wait for you," Feister said.

Silence descended again.

After a door opened and closed, Feister said, "Take a seat next to your sister."

"Are you okay?" Colleen asked gently in a soft-soothing tone.

"You know it wasn't my fault." April's voice still quivered.

"What happened, April?" Feister asked.

"Mark was high on cocaine."

"And were you?"

"April, the police are there," Colleen said. "Things are going to get worse. You better tell him everything, or do you want me to?"

"Georgina, tell me what happened, and don't leave anything out," Feister snapped.

"Well...a...a."

"For heaven sakes, I'll tell him," Colleen said.

"Mark was there when we showed up on Friday, but his car wasn't anywhere around."

"His car?" Feister said. "April, did you take back your Corvette?"

"No."

"When I said his car, I meant the Corvette. We asked how he got to the cabin. He claimed he walked. Mark seemed angry and agitated. He broke a chair on the porch."

"Did he stop taking his meds?"

"April asked him about that. He shrugged her off. We all thought that might be the problem. But later, he joked and laughed with us, even barbequed the steaks. Things were going good. That changed late Saturday afternoon when he pulled some guns out of a bush."

"Guns? Where did they come from?"

"Mark wouldn't tell us. He acted like someone had just left them in the bush."

"Pistols, rifles?"

"One of each. He lined up a row of cans on a log and shot at them."

"The guns were loaded?"

"Yes. And there also was a box of bullets in the bush. Each time Mark missed his target, he laughed, and we laughed with him. But after shooting off over a dozen bullets and not hitting any of the cans, he got mad and insisted that April should try doing better. He pushed the pistol in her hand, and it went off."

"It wasn't my fault," April pleaded.

"You shot Mark. Then what happened."

"Jared tried to save him," Georgina said. "But he

couldn't."

"And why didn't he report it?"

"Well…"

"I was high," April confessed. "We were all high except Jared and Colleen. I begged him not to report it."

"High on cocaine?…I see."

"Georgina, you were in agreement with him not reporting it?"

"I also begged him not to."

"All of you begged him to remain silent. I can understand April and Colleen swaying him not to report the gunshot wound, but Georgina, why were you begging him? I'm missing something."

"Georgina," Colleen said. "It'll eventually come out…Come on, Georgina… Mark was shot more than once."

"Like April said, we were all high," Georgina said. "I can't even remember picking up the rifle, but it ended up in my hand and just went off. The bullet skimmed Malcolm's arm and hit Mark. Had April not brought the cocaine, none of that would have happened."

Was that an accident? Georgina didn't seem that upset that Malcolm had left her. Had she seized an opportunity to get rid of him—permanently—but she lacked the skill to hit the intended target in a vital organ?

"I didn't force you to take it." Anger was evident in April's voice. "And I didn't bring the guns."

"Two bullets?" Feister said. "Colleen, where's Mark buried."

"By the cabin. Father, Jared tried to save him," she sniffled. "We're all to blame why he didn't report it.

He could lose his license. I don't care what happens to me, but can you help him so his license isn't taken away?"

That sounded like Colleen loved her cheating husband, a man who ignored her.

"He's just as much to blame as we are," Georgina snapped. "He should have reported it. It's the law. He shouldn't be given any special consideration."

Wow. Her true colors shined through. I thought she couldn't live without the man. *She doesn't want him to go unscathed.* Maybe she had the attitude if she couldn't have him, no one should. She wouldn't want him roaming the streets as a free man if she ended up being locked up.

Sobs continued in the background.

"There...there, dear. Jared won't lose his license," Feister said gently.

"But how?" Colleen's voice trembled.

"Don't worry about it. He'll be fine."

"What about me?" April asked.

"You're another matter," Feister said in a stern tone. "A man is dead and buried. That's new territory...April, you promised you'd seek help with your drug problem...Are there any illegal drugs at the cabin?"

"No."

"Did you use all you brought, or did you take some home with you?"

"The cabin is clean, and so is my house and car. The remaining cocaine is well hidden."

"Did you hide it in the hospital?"

"No...no, I'd never do that. And I only do drugs when I'm partying. It's not like I have a fix every day or anything like that. I've got it under control."

"If you had it under control, you wouldn't be dealing with this problem."

"But he pushed the gun into my hand."

"This can't be swept away. You'll need to talk to an attorney to determine how you're going to handle the questioning, but don't lie, especially to the police. I have no tolerance for any more lies spewing out of your mouth. And I don't want your problem spilling over into the hospital. Consider yourself on leave until the police close the case. How could you have dragged your sister into your mess again? Now get out of my office!" he barked.

"And what should I do?" Georgina asked.

"Get an attorney and leave the hospital. You're also not welcome here until the case is closed."

"But...but..."

"You could've said no to drugs at the cabin. Get out!"

"Do you want me to go too?" Colleen asked.

"No."

A door opened and closed.

"When the police discover the body, which I'm sure they will, I anticipate they'll want to question all of us...Lie down in there and rest. Phillip should be here soon."

"Your attorney."

"Yes. I'm going to call Jared. I want everyone to tell the truth. It won't look good if those at the cabin that weekend keep changing their stories based on what others have told the police."

"Thank you, Father. I feel so much better, like I can breathe again."

"I'm a little disappointed you didn't come to me earlier...No need to justify. I already figured it was because of your sister. You have to stop letting April lean on you."

"It's so hard."

"April is a fine doctor, but she has to learn how to manage her personal life. Neither you nor I are helping her if we continue to solve her problems. I better call Jared before the police do."

From everything I had heard about Feister, along with the few minutes I had spent with him in his office, I had the impression he was a stern, hard man who had risen to the CEO of Feister Northwest Hospital because of his birthright. After listening to him talk to the three women, my opinion of him changed. He was a smart, capable man who deserved to be respected. He cared about his daughters and the hospital.

My cell rang. Seeing the caller was Tucker, I flipped my device to record only and answered, "Have you found the body?"

"Yes. Buried near the spot you told me about. The guns were wrapped in plastic next to his body."

"Wrapped in plastic?"

"Yeah. They're on the way to the lab to check for fingerprints."

"What do you think? Whoever buried them wanted the guns to remain in good condition in case they planned to use them again? Or, since there were five people there, could it be to preserve the fingerprints so the wrong person wouldn't be suspected?"

"The body was also wrapped in plastic. Having the guns wrapped might not mean anything at all."

"What about the Corvette?"

"It's been discovered. According to Mark

Holbrook's apartment manager, he drove a red Corvette. Did you hear anything interesting?"

"Yep. Know who the shooters were."

"You know he was shot twice?"

"Yes. The first shot was an accident, but I'm not sure about the second one."

"Who shot him?"

"Let's talk later. I want to check on something before kids get out of school."

"Try not to get caught breaking in."

"I never have," I said, thinking about little Maci, but she caught me breaking out, not in.

Chapter 13

Georgina's blue Lexus was parked in her driveway when I reached her house. I had intended to read more of her journal entries to see if she'd mentioned something about wanting to kill her husband. I just couldn't buy that she suddenly found herself holding a rifle and it accidently discharged, the bullet grazing her husband first before it struck Mark. The incident at the cabin might not have any bearing on Sheila's case, but I still wanted answers. If there was anything incriminating written in Georgina's journal and with the police closing in, she might decide to tear out more pages.

On that thought, I slipped out of the car, grabbed my backpack, and cautiously moved into her backyard. To prevent the gate from squeaking, I climbed over it and made my way to the tree abutting the house. I quickly scaled up it and found the window locked. While I sat perched on a branch, preparing to clamber down, I glanced into the neighboring yard to make sure Maci wasn't watching me.

The slamming of drawers and a loud voice came from inside the house. Perking up my ears, I realized the voice belonged to Georgina. I picked up her angry tone but couldn't make out her words. *Is she on the phone or talking to herself?*

I spotted her entering her bedroom and ducked to the side so she couldn't see me.

"It has to be here somewhere," Georgina said as another drawer slammed shut.

The sound of a phone ringing blared through the windowpane.

"Hello, Jared," Georgina answered, standing next to the window. "When?...Yes, he called me in...April and Colleen spilled everything to the old man...Not yet. I begged him to help you so you wouldn't lose your license. He said he would."

What a liar! Taking credit for Colleen's unselfish pleas to her father. Will Feister tell Jared anything about Colleen coming to his defense, or will Georgina get away with her lie?

Georgina went on. "...No... Yes, she told the old man that she'd hidden the drugs...No, not at the cabin, her house, car, or the hospital...No, she wouldn't pin it on her sister. Your place is clean...Someplace where they could be retrieved. Otherwise, why hide the stuff? Just flush it down the toilet...Probably at my house the day she broke in.... Yes, I'm going to search every nook and cranny...Nothing was mentioned about Sheila...I'll be there."

Wondering if Georgina would be able to find the cocaine, I kept an eye on the neighbor's yard while I stayed in the tree and listened to rummaging, cracking, scrapping, slamming noises as she searched.

Georgina chuckled.

That piqued my curiosity. I leaned forward and carefully peered through the corner of the window and saw the bottom drawer of her dresser lying on the carpet. I couldn't see Georgina's face, which also meant she couldn't see me, but I saw her hands pick up the drawer and slide it back into the dresser. She stood up, brushed herself off, and began to turn around. I angled away from the window.

Heels clicking on a hard surface came next, signaling Georgina had either gone into the bathroom or into the hallway. The two possibilities were quickly cleared up when the clicking sound descended the stairwell.

Not hearing a toilet flush upstairs, I speculated about what Georgina planned to do with the white powder. Would she wash it down the kitchen sink? To find out, I climbed down from my perch and headed toward the kitchen window. The back door suddenly flew open. I charged toward the tree, ducked behind it, and observed Georgina put a white plastic bag into the garbage can near the gate and return to the house.

After waiting a few minutes, I tugged on a pair of latex gloves and then crept toward the garbage can and pulled out the white plastic bag. I carried it to a spot on the other side of the tree, a place where she wouldn't be able to easily spot me if she stepped out the backdoor again.

Inside the bag were plastic-wrapped syringes with needles attached and a container that looked like the one that had been in her bathroom fridge on my prior visit. Thinking it might be empty, I shook it. Hearing a rattling sound, I raised the lid and saw the vials of insulin. On my prior visit to her house, I didn't know who was a diabetic—Georgina or her husband. Since she was tossing it out, it must be him. I figured he had left the insulin behind, and she didn't want anything of his in the house. Still, throwing out needed insulin seemed strange. Maybe she thought he'd be running out of the supply he took with him soon. If he came back to get it when he desperately needed the medicine, he could end up in really bad shape. Feeling sorry for the unwanted husband, I decided to take the discarded bag and find a way to get the insulin to him without disclosing how I'd acquired it.

Leaving the bag hidden between the tree and the house, I went to the kitchen window and carefully peeked through it. Georgina was nowhere in sight. On the kitchen counter sat a purse with a striped sack sticking out of it that looked like the one April had hidden under Georgina's bottom dresser drawer. I crouched down when Georgina appeared in the kitchen doorway.

As I crept back to the tree, a car engine roared to life. To verify Georgina was taking off, I hurried to the corner of the house and looked toward the street. Her Lexus pulled out of the driveway and drove away. With the cocaine in her purse, was Georgina going to plant it in April's house? Or had she intended to plant it in the hospital where it could easily be found in order to get even with Feister for suspending her?

At any rate, she wasn't carrying a bug, so I wouldn't be able to quickly locate her, and I still wanted to have another look at her journal. After breaking in and disabling the alarm, I headed to Georgina's bedroom, pulled it out of her nightstand drawer, and turned to the last page. She had written every detail about the time she had spent with Jared, some of it quite graphic. I found myself staring at her last sentence. "I think I've convinced Jared to suspect that Colleen was the guilty person for drugging his precious Sheila."

Obviously, Georgina didn't care for Sheila, but why was she trying to pin the drugging onto Colleen? Did she believe Colleen might be responsible? Or was it to put more distance between Jared and Colleen than already existed?

Then I flipped back to a couple of weeks before April's birthday and began skimming through the entries for any mention of Malcolm. A few times she said how he didn't compare to Jared in any way. When I reached August 19th , four days before the cabin weekend trip, I caught the words insulin and Malcolm and read her entry. "Malcolm is a cheat and now wants to be with her. That's not going to happen. Too much insulin will also take care of that problem." That certainly confirmed she wanted him dead. Since he was still kicking, why had she thrown out his insulin?

I continued thumbing through the journal and noticed a few more pages had been torn out. Why hadn't she torn out August 19th? Was it just an oversight?

The next time Malcolm appeared was in her Sunday night entry. She wrote that Malcolm wanted to make their separation permanent. She went on and complained that he only took the children to dinner, not to a movie and dinner, which ruined her chance to have any private time with Jared.

I shook my head, thinking she wrote as if she were crazy about the guy, and yet she had no problem throwing him under the bus with everyone else. I couldn't help but think Malcolm had to of at least sensed that his wife was pining for Jared. Maybe that's what drove him away from Georgina, and he found love elsewhere with a woman who wanted to be with him. Georgina had lied to Jared, claiming Malcolm left her because of the cabin incident. Did Malcolm suspect the bullet that grazed his arm was meant for him?

Before putting away the journal, I pulled out my cell and snapped a picture of her August 19th entry about the insulin and the last entry in her journal where she tried to pin Sheila's drugging onto Colleen.

Next, I headed into the bathroom and checked the medicine cabinet for the unmarked pill containers. The one that held Ativan was gone. Gazing at the spot where it had once stood, I recalled some of Ativan's potential side effects were dizziness, loss of balance, and blurred vision. Had Sheila been given a large dose of Ativan? Was that why she swayed and staggered?

Chapter 14

When I arrived home, I fast forwarded the recording to the place where Colleen cried about Jared possibly losing his license and pleading with her father to help him. Feeling Jared needed to know the truth about who had come to his defense, I copied that section, which included Georgina saying Jared shouldn't go blameless, to a disk. Since Jared would be questioned about what went on at the cabin, I didn't want him to hear anything else said at the meeting. I slipped on a pair of gloves, put the disk into a mailer and printed three labels—one with the name Dr. Jared Ebert on it and two with the word "confidential" on it. After affixing them to the mailer, I put it in my backpack, intending to find a way to personally deliver it to Jared.

With that task done, I fast forwarded the recording again to April and Georgina leaving Feister's office, and played it. Feister told Colleen that instead of

Phillip, his attorney, coming to the hospital, he was going there, and he'd called Jared and would be meeting at his office later. Irritated that neither meeting would take place in Feister's office, I clicked on the recording associated with the bug planted on Colleen's purse. Except for the call she had with April, only garbled voices came through. Nothing else. After Feister called her, she probably rushed home, changed clothes, and switched purses before going to the hospital. That made sense. Showing up in a yoga outfit would undoubtedly not please her father.

While I made notes and contemplated how to get the insulin to Malcolm, my cell rang. "Hey, Maddie."

"Hi, Dora. Relatives have been calling to find out when the funeral will be. I've been trying to learn when the medical examiner is going to release Sheila's body. I feel like I'm getting the run around. Is that because of the drugs? Do they have to put someone behind bars before she can be buried?"

"Let me see what I can find out."

"Have you figured out who killed her?"

"I'm getting close but not there yet. How are you doing?"

"Tobias is so sweet. He makes breakfast for me before he goes to school and then comes home and cooks dinner. All I do is sleep and watch television. It's like all my energy has been sapped." She inhaled deeply. "I better let you go so you can hunt down the murderer."

When the call ended, I tapped on Tucker's number.

"Hey," he answered.

"Are you still at the cabin?"

"No. I'm at the precinct. The crime scene is still

being worked. Stan and I had expected someone to show up representing Feister, but no one did."

"After chatting with his daughters and Georgina, he probably decided to let it play out. I have a recording you might be interested in and a few pictures."

"That's how you picked up the identity of the shooters?"

"You got it."

"You home?"

"Yep."

"On my way."

Shortly before 6:00 p.m., Tucker walked into the house and strolled into the den. "Who are the shooters?" he asked, flopping down into a chair.

"The first was April." Then I summarized the meeting. "You'd probably prefer to listen to the whole recording."

As it played, Tucker scribbled down notes. When it clicked off, he said, "April's fingerprints were in the system and found on the pistol along with Mark Holbrook's. There wasn't a match in the system for the other set of prints on the rifle. Now I get why you suspect the bullet discharged from it wasn't an accident, but it could have been. Or at least, Georgina Levin will claim it was. Without any other proof, that might stick."

"But I do have other proof. Before I show it to you, Maddie called. She's getting the run around about when Sheila's body is going to be released. What gives?"

Tucker gazed at me for a minute.

"Come on. Spill it. You've already said the medical examiner found drugs in her system. Does he think she took them herself?"

"That possibility hasn't been ruled out, but since the tox report from the hospital didn't show any signs of drugs in her system, it appears suspicious. The medical examiner determined, besides drugs, Sheila had elevated insulin in her blood. It was so high that she wouldn't have been able to even walk after the injection. Dee, Sheila's cause of death wasn't the accident. She died from insulin intoxication."

"Sheila didn't walk in a straight line, but she made it to the street." I tilted my head and squinted. "Are you telling me that someone shot her up with insulin after the car accident?"

A contemplative expression flashed on Tucker's face as he nodded. "Yes."

"Remember, I wondered about the actual tox report after the first time I bugged Georgina and Jared. They talked like she had been murdered. And before that, I overheard Jared speaking to Sheila's dead body in the morgue. He had seen her blood reports—the tox report and the other one. The cardiac surgeon certainly knew what they meant."

I went to my printer, lifted up two pictures, and handed one to Tucker. "That's from Georgina's journal. It shows she wanted to get rid of her husband. She planned to kill him with insulin. That method could easily have been used to kill someone else she wanted out of the way. And when I was visiting her place today…"

Tucker rolled his eyes.

"…She dumped a plastic bag in her garbage. Guess what? It held vials of insulin. I thought her husband might be a diabetic, and she wanted to throw away his medicine. Now, I doubt he is. Killing someone with insulin and leaving a supply of it at her house wouldn't be too swift. And Georgina isn't dumb. April saw her in the emergency room right after Sheila was brought in. She thought Georgina was responsible for drugging Sheila. April probably didn't have a clue that Georgina showed up to finish the job."

Tucker read over the journal entry. "Also, Georgina Levin wrote 'Too much insulin will *also* take care of that problem.' That sounds like she might have used that method before. Are you aware of any other recent deaths among hospital personnel?"

"Maddie *did* say that Vicky Marsh, a former friend of Sheila's died from a rock climbing accident. They weren't getting along when that happened. Maddie also mentioned that Vicky might have had an affair with Jared."

"Did she die in the hospital?"

I nodded.

He rubbed his chin. "Interesting."

From the thoughtful expression on his face, I knew Vicky Marsh's death would be scrutinized.

Tucker held up the journal entry picture. "This sheds more light on both Mark Holbrook's and Sheila Wilson's cases, but it's not admissible evidence." He pulled out his cell. "Stan needs to get another search warrant before she tosses out her journal and the garbage is picked up."

I held up my hand in a stop motion. "The bag of insulin vials is in my trunk. Since I thought it was needed medicine, I had intended to give it to Georgina's husband. Georgina has already torn out a bunch of journal pages. She probably missed that one, but she could correct that mistake at any time."

"The bag can be returned to the garbage can when Stan gets a search warrant. Did you handle it without wearing gloves?"

"Nope. Always had them on."

"Bring the bag inside while I call Stan."

I nodded, put on a pair of latex gloves, and headed to my car. When I returned with the bag, Tucker was still talking on the phone. I went and grabbed two sodas from the fridge.

Laying his cell on the desk, Tucker said, "Earlier today, Stan mentioned that the convenience store owner confirmed Georgina and Malcolm Levin had been at the cabin that weekend. On the way there, they stopped and picked up a case of beer at the store. He also recalled seeing April filling up her gas tank on that Sunday."

"That guy doesn't miss anything, does he?"

"Maybe out-of-towners don't drop by very often." Tucker smiled at me. "He remembered you coming by and asking for directions to Feister's. Described you to a tee. When Stan got back to the office, an unidentified caller had left him a voice message claiming that Georgina Levin was a drug dealer."

I cocked my eyebrows. "Really? Georgina was high that weekend, but a dealer?…Maybe April is trying to pin everything on Georgina."

"Can't be her. Caller was a male. Disguised his voice, but not enough to hide his gender."

"How did Stan end up with the call?"

Tucker shrugged. "He's been making the rounds, searching for Mark Holbrook. He's left a card everywhere he frequents. Stan figures the anonymous caller has a connection to him."

"My guess would be Malcolm Levin. The first time

I overheard a conversation between Georgina and Jared, she said he blames her for what happened that weekend. And it sounded like he was stressed out. Maybe he wants the truth to surface and decided to point Stan in her direction under the façade of another crime."

"Possibly, but it might help Stan obtain a search warrant."

"Well, he won't find any drugs there. Georgina found them and took them someplace. My guess would be April's house."

"The first call Stan made at the precinct was to April Holbrook, informing her that her husband's body had been found. He's going to question her tomorrow. If she obeys her father's orders and tells the truth, that case will swiftly move along." Tucker gazed at the bag on the floor. "Let's see if we can locate any identifying purchase marks on the vials."

As he tugged on a pair of gloves, I took the container out of the bag, and then we started looking over the contents.

Tucker found a small sticker on the bottom of one of the vials. "I recognize this emblem. Towne Pharmacy. There are three or four in the city. That gives us a start. Have you got a picture of Georgina?"

"Yes." I pulled up the photo on my cell phone and showed it to Tucker. "I snapped this when I saw her at the hospital. I'll print off a couple."

"Thanks," Tucker said as I handed him the printed pictures. "I'll start asking questions in the morning. You need a badge to get info from pharmacies. You're going to have to sit that one out."

"Figured as much."

Chapter 15

After breakfast, Tucker placed a call to Stan. Stan told him that he wasn't able to secure a search warrant. Next, he called the medical examiner and found out that it would be several more days before Sheila's body would be released. Then he contacted the trash company that serviced Georgina's area. There he received some good news—garbage pick-up in Georgina's neighborhood was scheduled for that day. It would be either late morning or early afternoon. We both knew that meant the contents in that trash container would be considered abandoned property once it was put out to be picked up. No search warrant would be needed to go through it.

I put my gloves back on, grabbed the bag of insulin, and drove to Georgina's. Her trash container wasn't on the curb. I glanced at my watch—8:35 a.m. Since Georgina no longer needed to report to work, she probably wasn't in a rush to drag it to the street.

Cautiously, I headed to her backyard with the bag, climbed over the gate, and dropped it in the garbage can. Then I crept behind the familiar tree and kept a watchful eye on the container.

About thirty minutes later, the back door opened. Georgina, wearing sweats and carrying a filled green plastic bag, stepped out of her house and went to the garbage can. I cringed when she looked inside, thinking she might have put more trash in it after I retrieved the bag of insulin, so the white bag shouldn't be on top. I sighed when she put the green bag in the container, closed the lid, and pulled the container out of the back yard.

I quietly moved to the edge of the house, peeked around the corner, and watched her place the trash container in the street next to the curb. As she started walking toward the gate, I hurried back to my preferred hiding spot and stayed put until the back door closed behind her.

Stealthily, I sneaked back to my car and stared at Georgina's trash container as I called Tucker. "The garbage bin is ready for your search."

"On my way."

I remained vigilant with my eyes focused on it until Tucker showed up. To my surprise, he had a uniformed policeman with him.

The minute his gloved hand raised the trash can lid, Georgina rushed out of the house, and I rolled down my window to listen.

"What do you think you're doing?" she shouted.

Tucker's mouth was moving, but, unlike Georgina, he wasn't shouting, so I couldn't catch what he was saying. He offered her his card.

She grabbed it and stormed back into the house.

Tucker began rummaging through the trash. Then I saw Maci running toward him. Her hands were swinging around in an animated motion, and then she pointed at her trash container. From my vantage point, I couldn't pick up anything she was saying.

"Maci," a woman, who I took to be Maci's mother, said loudly, hurrying toward her and Tucker. She took Maci's hand and said a few words to Tucker and then walked Maci into her house.

As I wondered what that was all about, Tucker lifted out the green bag and the white one. He untied the white bag and looked in it, and then he handed the bag to the uniformed officer. While the officer put it in the trunk of Tucker's police car, Tucker sifted through the green bag and pulled out several crumbled up papers. He unfolded them and read each one.

Would Georgina be careless enough to throw incriminating documents, maybe pages of her journal, into the garbage? Doesn't she own a paper shredder? If not, why didn't she at least rip them up? Then I figured she probably had no idea that anyone was on to her. Or maybe she thought no one would come snooping around until the police started questioning everyone who had been at the cabin that weekend. And she had no idea that Sheila's body was at the medical examiner's lab and the police were searching for her murderer.

* * *

Sitting at my desk, I scribbled down some notes about my morning adventure to Georgina's house while I waited to hear from Tucker. He promised he'd let me know if he found out anything at the pharmacies and tell me how April's questioning went.

At 4:00 p.m., my patience had run out, and I called him. Voice mail answered. Before I could leave a message, my cell peeped, and Tucker's name appeared on the screen.

"Hey."

"We're getting close."

"How close?" I said, knowing that the insulin would make Georgina a prime suspect, but that wouldn't be enough to put her behind bars.

"I'm on my way home. We'll talk when I get there."

Within ten minutes, Tucker strolled into the den and sank down into a chair and leaned back. "I feel like it's been a long day, and it's not even five."

"You said you were getting close to solving Sheila's murder."

"We are. The first pharmacy I hit, the one farthest from her house, both the pharmacist and a store clerk recognized the picture. When Georgina Levin was there, she gave the pharmacist a bad time about taking so long to fill the prescription. Not cool if you want to stay under the radar. Dr. Raymond Feister was the prescribing doctor. I had the pharmacist call him to substantiate the prescription. Feister hasn't ever prescribed any medications for Georgina, and he knew she wasn't a diabetic. He asked the pharmacist to send him a copy of the prescription. The pharmacist immediately complied and faxed Feister a copy."

"You know that means he'll never let Georgina work for him," I snickered.

"Georgina Levin might not need a job for quite a while. Besides the insulin in her garbage, she also threw out some documents she should've burned."

"Yeah, I saw you pulling some paper out. Pages out of her journal?"

"Several came from it, including the one you snapped a picture of. There was also a life insurance policy on her husband, dated ten days before the weekend trip to the cabin. She had acquired the policy without her husband's knowledge. The agent who sold it to her said her husband was sick in bed when he went to their house for his signature. The agent believes Georgina had her husband sign it in the bedroom while he waited in their living room."

"Were her kids there?"

"The house was quiet when he arrived, and he never saw any children there."

"So her plan was to kill off her husband and make a few bucks in the process."

"A million bucks."

"I wonder how she knew Mark Holbrook was going to show up at the cabin with guns. Maybe she intended to use insulin that weekend."

"Perhaps when Mark told the group that he just found the guns in the bushes, it might have been the truth. Georgina wasn't at work the Wednesday before the party weekend. We're trying to determine who bought or acquired the weapons. Neither weapon is new. That could present a problem in locating the purchaser. I sat in while Stan questioned April about that weekend. She was accompanied by an attorney. She told how the events unfolded, leaving out any mention of drug usage. With that exception, her story jived with the one you had recorded."

"Did you ask her any questions about Sheila?"

"Yes, when Stan was through, I asked her

questions about the night Sheila Wilson was brought into the emergency room. Before I finished my first question, she spit out that Georgina Levin had come to see Ms. Wilson and stayed by her side until Sheila was taken to surgery. As a follow-up, I asked if Georgina had been left alone with Sheila. From April's expression, that question puzzled her, but she admitted there was a brief moment the two were alone while she was on the phone with the surgeon."

"Maybe she was concerned about malpractice, as if she hadn't provided Sheila with competent medical care."

"Hadn't thought about that. April volunteered that Georgina was after her brother-in-law and Sheila and Georgina weren't friends. She couldn't understand why Georgina insisted on staying in the ER with Sheila."

"She just volunteered the information?"

"Yeah. That seemed suspicious. April's a doctor. More than likely, she saw the real blood reports and knows the actual cause of death."

"Since you questioned her about Sheila, she now knows Sheila's death is being investigated, something she might have doubted would happen. April could've learned that Sheila, her friend, was having an affair with her brother-in-law and was pleased that Georgina had taken care of the problem. But when you started questioning her about it, she wanted to point you in the right direction."

"Or she could be protecting her sister. You mentioned that Georgina had told Jared that Colleen was in the hospital that day."

"Good point."

"If April's statement about Georgina being in the

ER can be substantiated, that along with Georgina's handwritten journal entries and the insulin will give us a motive, opportunity, and means. But that evidence won't be enough to prove she's the guilty party. As far as her journal is concerned, people often write things they have no intention of doing. The most damaging piece of evidence we have is the insulin. Georgina purchased 20 vials. There were only 16 in the plastic container in her garbage. Her popping up with the other four will wipe out that evidence. Did you see any more at her house?"

"I never looked in her kitchen fridge. But with kids in the house, I doubt she'd put any in there. Given the level of insulin in Sheila, did the medical examiner say how much would have been injected?"

"I intend to discuss that with her tomorrow."

"What can I help with?" I asked, wondering how I could track down a list of nurses and doctors who were working the ER the night Sheila was brought in.

"Malcolm Levin is scheduled to come to the station tomorrow morning and Jared Ebert in the afternoon regarding the Mark Holbrook case."

"No mention about Sheila?"

"No, but they will be questioned about her."

"By now, I'm sure April has already given her sister and, possibly her father, a complete run down on everything you and Stan questioned her about. Jared will know Sheila was discussed."

"Yes, but the real cause of death was never mentioned."

"Yeah. Even though we suspect she knows, I can't imagine she'd confess that to her father. She's already in enough hot water with him."

"That's exactly how I see it. Also tomorrow, I'll be

making some inquires at the hospital in the administration department. Someone there might be able to provide some valuable information about Georgina Levin. In addition to having more witnesses who can testify that she was interested in Jared Ebert, we also need witnesses who can testify that Ebert was involved with Sheila at the time of her death."

"To start with, there's Maddie and Tobias. They both know Jared and Sheila were having an affair. I'll get more names from Maddie. How about the motel? Maybe the clerk can recall seeing Jared and Georgina."

"That's already on my list. Whoever was on duty might be able to say they shared a room. Not staying the whole night makes it look like a lovers' rendezvous. That will show their relationship was more than Georgina just being interested in Jared."

Tucker's cell rang. He pulled it out of his pocket and headed into the hallway.

While he was gone, I jotted down a list of what I intended to work on. Finding a way to deliver the disk to Jared was on top of it. Thinking he might try to defend Georgina if something was mentioned about her in the interview at the police department, I wanted him to hear it before he went.

Dropping his cell in his pocket, Tucker strolled back into the kitchen. "A homicide. I need to go."

"What about dinner?"

"I'll grab something later."

"Oh…Oh, before you leave, what did Maci say to you when you were going through Georgina's trash can?"

"Maci?"

"The 3- or-4-year-old little brunette."

Tucker chuckled. "She told me we could take whatever we wanted out of her garbage can because her mom didn't want it anymore."

I laughed. "She must have seen Georgina arguing with you about it."

"That's what I assumed. Cute kid. Got to go."

As the door closed behind him, I checked my watch—5:03 p.m. Jared would be heading home soon. Thinking this might be a good time to leave the disk on his desk, I key-punched a note and printed it. It read: "Urgent. Listen to this disk ASAP!"

Before removing it from the printer, I retrieved my oversized purse and slipped on a pair of gloves and then stuck the note, the mailer, and a few other items from my backpack into the purse. I headed into my bedroom, changed into my nurse's uniform and gathered up a couple of pairs of oversized glasses. After putting them in the purse, I worked on my face to make myself look at least twenty years older, so I wouldn't be easily identified. Satisfied with my makeup job, I tucked my hair into a bob-styled auburn wig.

Chapter 16

Driving into the hospital parking lot, my eyes drifted around, searching for Jared's white Porsche. Not seeing it anywhere, I pulled my listening device out of my purse and looked for the location of the bug planted in his car. I pressed my lips together and shook my head, seeing the white Porsche was parked in front of Georgina's house. That reinforced my conviction that he had to hear the disk—the recording of Colleen pleading for him and Georgina wanting him to suffer with everyone who had been at the cabin when the fatal shots were fired.

When I reached Jared's medical offices, I tried the door. Like I had expected, it was locked. I could easily break in using my picks, but I hesitated, thinking an alarm would blare the second the door opened. A cleaning cart full of cleaning supplies stood in the hallway a few doors away. Figuring a cleaning crew was close, I strolled toward the cart as another one was pushed out of an office into the hallway by a janitor in his early thirties.

"Are you going to be cleaning all of the offices on this floor," I asked, waving my hand toward them.

"Yes. If there is something unusual you'd like us to clean, you'll have to talk to my boss."

"No. That's not it. I left my cell phone in Dr. Ebert's office and I don't have a key. Can you let me in to get it?"

"Let me check." He went back into the office he had just left, and I heard him say, "Marge, a woman left her cell phone in one of the offices. Can I let her in to get it?"

"I'll handle it."

An overweight, fifty-something woman stepped into the hallway. "Which office?"

"Dr. Ebert's."

She walked toward his office with me right behind her. The woman unlocked his door. No alarm sounded when she opened it. Probably having the door opened with a proper key disarmed it. She stood in the doorway as I walked through his reception area and down the hallway lined with examination rooms. Toward the back was a door with a name plate on it—Dr. Jared Ebert. To my chagrin, it was locked. Moving as quickly as possible I grabbed my picks and unlocked it.

"Can't you find it?" the woman yelled.

"Just need to check one more place," I said loudly, tugging a glove on. I pulled the disk out of my purse, placed it on the center of his desk, and put the note on top of it. I flipped the lock on his door, hurried out, and shut the door.

"No luck." With my hands behind my back, I

removed the glove as I strolled toward the woman. "I know I left it here. Maybe one of the other nurses stuck it in a cabinet. I'll make some calls when I get home. Thank you so much for letting me in," I said, walking out into the main hallway after the woman. "I really appreciate it."

She smiled. "I hope you find your cell."

"So do I. Thanks again." I turned on my heel and walked to the bridge that connected the medical building to the hospital.

Doubting Georgina had cleared all of her belongings out of the administrative department since her departure had been presented as a temporary leave, I wanted to check out her desk.

Two nurses, one in her thirties and the other middle-aged, were chatting near the ER double doors while I walked toward the corridor leading to the administration department. When I was within earshot, the middle-aged nurse glanced at me. With my thick rimmed glasses, makeup, and auburn hair, it was unlikely that I looked familiar, but I recognized her from the night Sheila was brought in. She was the nurse that wouldn't allow me to enter the ER because I wasn't a relative.

"Are you sure?" the middle-aged nurse said to the younger one.

"Yes, Dr. Holbrook grabbed all of her stuff and left. She's done something."

As I passed them, I caught the first name on the thirty-something's badge—Christie. Knowing they were talking about April's quick departure, I slowed my pace and then came to a stop, lowered my purse to the floor, and rummaged through it.

"Maybe someone has filed a malpractice suit."

Christie said, "Did you tell anyone about, you know? I don't want to get canned."

"We need to get back."

I glanced over my shoulder in time to see them going through the door to the ER. The clock near it showed—6:36 p.m. Was Christie also working the evening Sheila was brought in?

Picking up my purse, I continued to the admin department while I mulled over what the young nurse could have done that would cause her to think she'd get fired if it was revealed. It probably had absolutely nothing to do with my case, but I intended to verify that.

Reaching the corridor to the admin department, I scanned for surveillance cameras, something I didn't need to worry about on my legitimate visits to that department. I spotted two cameras near the ceiling. One pointed to the administration department double doors. In my purse was a spray can of gray paint, a color that didn't automatically stand out like the color black would, but did an effective job of disabling surveillance cameras up to ten feet away from me. *Is there a person or two at the hospital constantly keeping track of the cameras*? I decided to give it a shot and see how it played out. Worst case scenario, I'd climb out of Feister's window. But before using my spray, I checked to make sure the admin door was locked. It was. In case someone was in there working, I pulled out my cell phone and called Georgina's office number. The sound of her phone ringing drifted through the door. After six rings, I hung up and glanced up and down the hallway. Not seeing anyone, I headed toward the surveillance camera. As I started to pull the spray can out of my purse, a well-dressed man carrying a briefcase came down the corridor. I again lowered my purse to the floor, pulled out my cell phone, and pretended to make a call as I waited for him to go by me, but instead he stopped in front of the administrative department.

He took a 9x12 envelope out of his briefcase and pushed it under the door. As he stood up, he looked my direction, and I felt him briefly scrutinizing me. Then he turned and walked away.

When he was out of sight, I quickly pulled the can out of my purse and directed the thin powerful spray at the surveillance camera. Some spots landed on the surrounding wall, but since the walls were gray, I didn't worry about it. Then I rushed to the admin door, quickly unlocked it, hurried in, and closed the door as the automatic lights flickered on. Relieved no alarm went off and keeping my head bent in case surveillance cameras were in the department, I saw the 9x12 envelope under my feet. I made a mental note to brush it off when I got a chance. Then I ducked down near a desk and scoped the room for surveillance cameras. Not seeing any, I quickly slipped on a pair of latex gloves, went to Feister's door, and using my picks, unlocked it in case an escape route was needed. Then I hunkered down by Georgina's desk and remained motionless but prepared to charge into Feister's office if I heard noise in the hallway or the sound of the lock cylinder clicking. Within ten minutes, the lights automatically turned off. I continued waiting another fifteen minutes in the dark. Only hearing the humming of a refrigerator, I figured the surveillance cameras in the corridor were not monitored 24/7. With my ears on high alert, I rose to my feet as the lights flickered on and picked up the envelope on the floor in front of the hallway door. As I brushed off my footprints on it, I noticed it was addressed to Dr. Raymond Feister, and the word "Confidential" was stamped on it a few times. My eyes moved to the return address—Phillip Statton and Associates, Attorneys of Law.

Intending to put it back on the floor when I left, I set it on the top of Georgina's desk. I gripped the handle of the center drawer. It was locked, which lead me to believe there might be something interesting in her desk. Using my picks again, I unlocked it.

The usual office supplies—pencils, pens, elastics, paperclips, glue sticks, notepaper —were in the center drawer and the left top drawers. The second drawer on that side of the desk held a pocket-sized medical terminology dictionary and blank forms. The bottom drawer appeared to be empty, but it stuck so I couldn't pull it out all the way. I guessed that was where she kept her purse during the day. Sticking my hand in the back of it, I felt a wrapper and lifted it out and saw it was a plastic-wrapped syringe with a needle attached. Her husband was still alive. *Does she keep it here in case an opportunity rises where she can change that?* But then, there had to be another vial of insulin nearby.

Mulling that over, I put back the syringe and moved to the drawers on the other side of her desk, two appointment books were in the top drawer. One contained Feister's scheduled appointments. Gazing at it, I couldn't resist and, with a smile on my face, I opened it to Thursday. His whole day was filled in. I went to the next day, Friday, eyed his appointments, and found he had an open period from 2:30 to 4:00 p.m. Doing my best to forge Georgina's handwriting,

I wrote Sally Richards in his 3:00 p.m. time slot. That was the name I used when I charged into his office to plant the bug. After Feister told me to make an appointment, he told Georgina never to give Sally Richards an appointment. That just wasn't right.

Feeling pleased with myself, I pulled out the other appointment book. It was smaller with Georgina's name on the cover. It included who she was meeting for lunch, drinks, places she was going shopping, doctor and dentist appointments, everything. *She must be a lot more organized than I am.*

Then recalling she told Jared that she had lunch with Colleen the day Sheila died, I sat down in her desk chair and thumbed through it until I reached the page that contained September 20th. She had a luncheon meeting that day with some admin employees. Georgina listed the names. None were familiar. Glancing through her appointments, I noticed that she often had lunch with April and occasionally with Colleen. So, what she had said to Jared about having lunch with Colleen that day was a lie, but that didn't rule out that Colleen could've been in the hospital the day Sheila died.

Next, I flipped to August 21st, the Wednesday before the birthday weekend, the day Tucker mentioned Georgina wasn't at work. That would have given her an opportunity to take the guns to the cabin if she had purchased them. It was also the same day April Holbrook had reported her husband missing. I stared at the entry in Georgina's appointment book— "meeting April for lunch, going shopping for sporting goods with her and on a long drive." "Sporting goods"—could that be guns? She never spelled where the long drive would take them. Still, it certainly made me wonder if they were in cahoots about what went down at the cabin. Maybe what happened to Mark Holbrook wasn't an accident at all. Did April know he'd be at the cabin and only reported him missing to cover her tracks? Was that why April had remained quiet about Sheila's cause of death—Georgina helps her out with her problem, and she helps Georgina out with hers? But when the police started asking questions about Sheila, April had no intention of allowing them to believe she might have been responsible. Assuming I was on the right track, didn't April think Georgina would also turn on her and tell the truth about the shooting? Her sister believed it was accident, and probably Jared and Malcolm Levin also believed that. Then they'd all testify it was an accident, discrediting anything Georgina said to the contrary. But if—that's a big if—April had purchased the guns that could lead them to doubt it was an accident. I pulled out my phone and snapped a picture of that page in Georgina's appointment book. Then I thumbed back to September 20th to check the time her last meeting or appointment was scheduled—nothing after 3 p.m.

I put her appointment book back into the drawer and began searching the file-sized drawer. Based on the labels on the files, it appeared they all had something to do with Feister—nothing personal. To verify that, I flipped through a few of them and then noticed there was a space between the files and the back of the drawer. Pulling the drawer out further, I reached behind the folders and pulled out a striped sack tucked behind them. Just feeling it, I knew it was the cocaine. Still, I looked in it. Did she hide it there for her own usage or to use as leverage if she wanted

Feister's help to deal with her legal problems? During the meeting, he was concerned that April might have hidden the cocaine in the hospital. Finding illegal drugs in Feister's hospital would be a black mark against its outstanding reputation. I had the urge to take it with me, but it could be used as evidence in the Mark Holbrook case, so it had to remain in place so that the police could find it. I pushed the sack back into the hiding spot, closed the drawer, and felt under the drawers, a habit I did whenever I searched a desk. Often interesting notes or keys were attached. Not finding anything like that, I locked her desk.

Before someone discovered the bug in Feister's office, I intended to retrieve it. Since the light would go on the minute his door was opened and the light could be seen in the parking lot, I wanted to look around for the insulin before venturing into his office.

Recalling the humming of a refrigerator, I figured the department had a break room. I stepped between two desks and tried the door a woman carrying a cup of coffee came out of on a prior visit. It opened with ease. Seeing it led to a break room, I stepped in and went to the fridge to search for any container that might have Georgina's name on it. She had two colorful plastic containers. Neither one was translucent. Whatever was inside would be well hidden from anyone looking into the fridge. One contained cubes of cheese. The other one held four vials of insulin. Four? The top seals weren't broken. I still held each one up to verify none of the liquid inside was missing. They were all full. The twenty vials Georgina had purchased were all accounted for. Feeling disappointment, I closed the container and put it back in the fridge. Could she have snatched one or two vials from the hospital supply?

As I headed toward Feister's office, my eyes drifted to the envelope from his attorney. After discussing the cabin problem with his daughters and Georgina, Feister had scheduled a meeting with his attorney. I wondered if the contents related to that meeting.

I took the envelope into the break room. Sitting on top of a two-burner unit was a tea pot. From its weight, I knew it held enough water to handle my task and turned on the burner. While the water heated up, I laid the envelope on the table and unlocked Georgina's desk again and took out a glue stick. Then I steamed open the envelope and lifted out the document inside. To my surprise, it wasn't about Mark Holbrook's death. It was about Sheila Wilson's toxicology report and the potential liability the hospital could face for releasing inaccurate information to the police department. Tucker never mentioned the hospital had been informed about the discrepancy, but that didn't mean they hadn't been informed. I made a mental note to check with him about it as I put the document back into the envelope and resealed it.

After putting the glue stick back in Georgina's desk and locking it, I went into Feister's office to recoup the bug. It wasn't on the windowsill. I knelt down on the floor to hunt for it and ran my fingers under his desk. No bug. With his office light shining out into the parking lot, I couldn't spend any more time looking for it and hurried out, closing his door behind me. I dropped the envelope on the floor where I'd found it and left the admin department. In the corridor, I looked up at the surveillance camera.

The gray paint still covered it.

Back in my car, I turned on my listening device and adjusted the dial to the bug that had been in Feister's office. I had hoped that it had been knocked on the floor, stepped on, and swept away by a cleaning person. No such luck. It showed it was functioning. Then I checked its location and recognized the address that appeared on the screen— Jared and Colleen Ebert's house. *Does she know who I am?*

Chapter 17

The following morning, I awoke as Tucker strolled out of the bathroom with a towel wrapped around his waist. My eyes focused on his well-built body. "You look mighty good. Care to come back to bed?"

"Can't. Need to get to the precinct."

I sat up and gazed at him as he dressed. "Hey, did you or the medical examiner call Feister or someone in the hospital to let them know the tox report for Sheila was wrong?"

"No one has called yet. The pathology department at Feister Northwest Hospital won't be informed until after Malcolm and Georgina Levin and Jared and Colleen Ebert have been interviewed."

"Well, Feister knows."

"How?"

I shrugged.

"And how do you know he knows?"

"Don't want to go into that."

"Any idea if he's shared that information with his daughters?"

Shaking my head, I said, "Nope. Oh, I found the four vials—unused."

"Where?"

"Fridge in admin department's break room. They were in a container with Georgina's name written on it. But it's possible she snatched some insulin from the hospital."

"Did you examine them for the Towne Pharmacy emblem?"

I shook my head, irritated with myself for not looking for it.

"Then it's also possible those vials weren't included in the twenty she purchased." He came and sat down on the edge of the bed and took my hand. "Did you find out anything else snooping around last night?"

Since Tucker sometimes thinks I go bug crazy, I had no intention of telling him that Colleen had swiped the one left in Feister's office. "Georgina hid the cocaine at the back of her bottom desk drawer—the drawer that's a file drawer."

"Interesting. After being dismissed, she must want to throw a shadow over the hospital."

"Or she might have thought that was the safest place to store it. Will you be getting a search warrant to look through her desk and files at her place of employment?"

"When we have enough evidence to substantiate obtaining one."

"I also discovered…I'll just show you." I grabbed my cell phone and clicked to a photo. Holding it up in front of him, I said, "That's from Georgina's appointment book."

He studied it. "You think April and Georgina are partners in crime?"

"I wouldn't rule it out."

Tucker squinted at the picture, and then he moved his fingers over it, making it larger. "Bo."

"Bo? What are you talking about?"

He pointed to the edge of the photo near Georgina's appointment with April. In parenthesis was the word "Bo." "You think that means something?" I asked.

"Maybe. A guy with the nickname Bo deals in stolen weapons."

"Why isn't he behind bars?"

He held up his hand with his palm facing me. "It's complicated."

With my eyes fixed on Tucker's face, I figured that Bo, whoever he was, sometimes gave valuable info to the police. Locking him up could be detrimental. "Does he file off serial numbers?"

"Sometimes. Not always. The rifle we dug up at Feister's cabin didn't have a serial number. The pistol did. It isn't registered and wasn't purchased from any legitimate retailer. We plan to expand our search. Bo's on that list." He gave me a quick kiss. "When I see you later, I'll let you know how the interviews went."

After slipping on a robe and pouring a cup of coffee, I placed a call to Maddie.

"Hey," she answered, "have you solved the crime?"

"Not yet, but I'm narrowing in. Besides you and Tobias, who else knew Sheila and Jared Ebert were having an affair?"

"She was kind of hush-hush about it, but a lot of

people knew. To tell you the truth, I think April might've known."

"Why do you think that?"

"Well...when I was in the waiting room, April sat next to me. She asked me if Jared knew about Sheila. Sheila worked on his surgical team, but there'd be no reason to contact him if that was it. I mean...she wasn't having heart surgery. April's question just struck me like she knew. I could be wrong, but that's what I think."

"Can you give me some names of people who knew for sure about their affair?"

"My boss for one. I'll put together a list and text it to you. How many names do you want?"

"Five...six...That should be enough."

"I'll get right on it."

"By any chance do you know a nurse in ER with the first name Christie?"

"Christie...you think she's somehow involved with what happened to Sheila?"

"No...No. I'm trying to figure out who else might have been working in the ER that evening."

"Christie Singer. She always jokes about her last name because she can't carry a tune. We had classes together and graduated in nursing the same year. Tell her that you and I are friends. Otherwise, she might be reluctant to talk to you.

"Will do."

"She works twelve hour shifts—7:00 a.m. to 7:30 p.m., three days a week, not the same days each week. I couldn't handle twelve hour shifts, but mothers really like it."

"Christie has children?"

"A three-year-old son. She's a single mom."

"Thanks for the info."

After we said our goodbyes, I went into the den, flipped on my computer, and searched for Christie Singer's address. She lived a few blocks from me. I glanced at the clock—8:20 a.m. If she had the day off, it was the perfect time to pay her a visit.

Within a half an hour, I climbed into my car and drove toward Christie's house. As I turned onto her street, I saw a row of well-maintained duplexes and fourplexes. Christie lived in a duplex.

I flew the strap of my backpack over my shoulder and headed to her door. Hearing voices through the door, I rang the doorbell.

A middle-aged woman answered. "Hello," she said with a smile.

"Oh, I must have the wrong address." Then a little boy edged next to the woman. "Does Christie Singer live here?"

"Yes." The woman swung around. "Christie, it's for you."

"Who is it, Mom?" Christie shouted from another room.

The woman turned toward me.

"I'm a friend of Maddie Wilson."

The woman relayed that information to her daughter. Then Christie, wearing sweats, strolled toward the door as her mother took the hand of the little boy and walked away.

"Have we met?" Christie asked, eyeing me up and down.

"I don't think so. My name is Dora Stephens. I'm a friend of Maddie's and looking into the death of her Aunt Sheila."

"What does that have to do with me? And her

Aunt died from a car crash. What's there to look into?"

Doubting she was on friendly basis with any of my prime suspects, I said, "To help out Maddie, if I tell you something about Sheila's death, can you keep it a secret?"

"I still don't see what this has to do with me," she said, sounding defensive.

"You were working in the ER when Sheila was brought in," I said, though I wasn't sure that was true.

"Are you implying I did something wrong in the ER?"

I held up my hand in a stop motion. "No. Absolutely not. Quite the contrary. Maddie thinks you're a wonderful nurse and completely honest. Sheila was drugged before she was hit by a car. I'm trying to figure out who drugged her," I said, not planning to say anything about the insulin.

Her eyes popped wide open. "Drugged? Really?"

"Yes."

"I don't want my son or mother to hear any of this. Let's sit on the steps," Christie said, walking out of the house.

Once we were settled, I asked, "Did you observe anything unusual in the ER regarding Sheila that evening—visitors, non-ER doctors, nurses, or administrators checking on her… anything?"

She pressed her lips together. "Well, there was an incident…but you can't tell anyone that I told you about it."

I ran my thumb and index finger across my mouth. "My lips are sealed. I'm a private investigator and skilled in keeping secrets."

Tilting her head, she squinted. "I thought you said

you were Maddie's friend."

"I am. Her best friend. I knew her before her parents' accident."

"Okay…when Dr. Holbrook was examining Sheila Wilson, her sister, Mrs. Ebert, showed up in the ER and they had words."

"Angry words?"

Christie nodded.

"Do you recall what was said?"

"Not every word, but it started when Dr. Holbrook shouted, 'What are you doing here, Colleen? Get out.' Mrs. Ebert said that Dr. Holbrook had told her to come. Then Dr. Holbrook said that she didn't have time to deal with Mrs. Ebert's problems. Mrs. Ebert just stared at her. Dr. Holbrook pointed to a chair and told Mrs. Ebert to sit down and they'd talk later. Then I noticed Mrs. Ebert looking at the patient like she recognized her."

"Was Mrs. Ebert ever left alone with Sheila Wilson?"

"Probably. Another patient came in. I had to attend to that patient, but I did see Dr. Holbrook talking on the phone and then giving instructions to two other nurses, so Mrs. Ebert must have been alone with Sheila."

"What other nurses attended to Sheila?" I asked, taking a notepad and pen out of my backpack. I jotted down the names as Christie gave them to me. Did you see anyone who wasn't working in the ER visiting or checking on Sheila?"

"No. No one else." She bit her lower lip and clutched her hands together.

I sensed she was holding something back. Did she see someone else there? Or did she see something she didn't dare talk about? "Anything else unusual happen in the ER while Sheila was there?"

Pressing her lips together, she shook her head.

Pulling out a business card, I said, "If you think of anything, will you give me a call?"

"Yes." She took the card.

"And I'd appreciate it if you didn't mention our conversation to anyone."

"I won't."

As we stood up, I reached out my hand and shook hers. "Thanks. You've been very helpful."

"When you see Maddie, tell her how sorry I am about her loss."

"I will, and I'll also let her know how helpful you've been."

Driving away, I ran the conversation I heard last night between Christie and another nurse over in my head. Was mentioning the angry words between April and Colleen the reason she was worried it could lead to her being fired? Or was it something entirely different? Everyone who worked in the ER knew April was Feister's daughter. Had rumors spread that they couldn't say anything negative about her without facing consequences?

Wanting to verify the bug was still at Colleen's house, I pulled into a strip mall parking lot, turned on my device, and clicked to it. The bug was no longer there, and I didn't recognize the address that appeared on the screen. Still, that was my next stop.

Chapter 18

Following my GPS directions, I made a right turn and found a closed gate in front of me. I clicked on my phone and searched for another way to reach my destination. There wasn't one. Knowing my bug was in a gated community, I flipped a U-ey and parked along the abutting street. Before footing it to the location, I checked my listening device to make sure the bug hadn't been moved again. Seeing it was in the same place, I studied its location on the map and then grabbed my backpack, climbed out of the car, and headed to the gate.

I climbed over it, meandered through a few streets, and turned into a cul-de-sac. Then I saw a gray Volvo parked in the driveway of the house where my bug was located. Guessing the house belonged to April, it surprised me that the modern-looking, one-story structure appeared to be appreciably larger than Colleen's house. At the same time, I liked that it was only one-story—much easier to escape. To get a better look at the white wrought-iron side gate, I slowly walked by and figured it would be a snap to climb over, but then I spotted a surveillance camera at the side of the house. She had a better security system than Georgina. That added an extra challenge to breaking into April's place.

Since she had been suspended from working at the hospital for the time being, I wondered if I'd have to hang around her neighborhood and wait for her to leave or if there was another way I could draw her away from her house. Assuming she didn't know who had planted the bug in her father's office, would she take it with her when she left? And why had it been at Colleen's house yesterday? Had Colleen found the bug and given it to her sister? Too many questions kept buzzing through my head as I headed back to my car.

Climbing into the driver's seat, I doubted April would be foolish enough to say anything within earshot of the bug. I still turned on the device and put the signal from that bug on record. Then I pulled out my cell phone and put on the volume. In the process, I saw one missed call, one voice mail, and two text messages—all from Tucker.

I clicked on his voicemail. All he said was "Call me." When I placed the call, it went immediately to voicemail and I said, "Returning your call." Tucker and I had an understanding that we would always leave a message if we called each other. No message meant we were in trouble. I always thought it was really a one-way agreement. If Tucker was in trouble, he had ways to contact his boss or another officer. I wouldn't be on top of his list, but he definitely was on top of mine. So I left him a message saying I was on my way home. Then I tapped on his texts. One read: "You're on the right track." The other: "Call me."

It was 3:12 p.m. when I arrived home. As I put away some groceries, my cell buzzed. Seeing it was Tucker calling, I answered, "Hey. How are the interviews going?"

"Malcolm Levin was a nervous wreck. Even confessed to calling Stan and saying his wife was a drug dealer. He thought if the police contacted her, it might make her think twice before she tried to kill him again."

"Again?"

"Yes. His recollection of the shooting jived with April Holbrook's, except he believes Georgina meant to kill him. He jerked away when he saw the rifle in her hands, pointed at him."

"That's what we both suspected."

"April never indicated that Malcolm might have been a target. Both April's and Malcolm's versions have been documented and recorded. According to the recording of the meeting in Feister's office, they were both high, but neither one mentioned that, and that recording isn't admissible. Based on that recorded meeting, Jared and Colleen Ebert weren't high. Jared Ebert's interview is scheduled for 4:00 p.m. Stan intends to drill him more about the specifics of the shooting. He's also set up interviews with Colleen Ebert and Georgina Levin for tomorrow.

"After Malcolm's interview, Stan and I paid a visit to Bo. I showed him a picture of Georgina Levin and asked if she was a customer. He remembered the attractive woman and confirmed that she had purchased a pistol with the serial number intact, along with a rifle and another pistol—no serial number."

"You thinking that there was a screw up and the wrong pistol was left at the cabin?"

Without answering my question, Tucker said, "He also said that another person was in the car when Georgina Levin purchased the weapons. With the tinted car windows, he couldn't make out any features but knew the passenger's hair was pulled back into a ponytail. The same hairdo April Holbrook had when she came to the precinct and reported her husband missing. Bo keeps receipts—no names, only dates and items purchased. In case problems arise, he wants to know the true identity of his customers and manages to get their fingerprints. The fingerprints match the unidentified set on the rifle."

"Glad to hear the illegal gun dealer knows how to run a business."

"The receipt was dated August 21st, the Wednesday before the cabin weekend. It coincides with the shopping expedition in Georgina's appointment book. Since you weren't home when I called, I assume you've been busy investigating. Find out anything interesting today?

"Maddie gave me the name of a nurse that was on duty in the ER when Sheila was brought in. I talked with her earlier today. She said that Colleen Ebert came to the ER when April was examining Sheila. April shouted at Colleen asking her why she was there and wanted her to get out and said something about she couldn't deal with Colleen's problems right then. Colleen said that April had asked her to come there. What do you think?"

"One is lying."

"Already figured that one out. The nurse also thinks that Colleen was left alone with Sheila. She couldn't be positive because at that time she was helping another patient. Besides ER personnel, no one else was near Sheila."

"April must have been trying to protect her sister when she volunteered that information about Georgina being there. What's the name of the nurse you spoke with?"

"I promised her I'd keep our conversation confidential. I think she's afraid of being fired if she says April had loud, angry words with her sister in the ER. I'm sure she knows April is Feister's daughter. But...but I sensed she was holding something back. Maybe that's what she was concerned about."

"Someone else might've showed up?"

"Possibly, but I don't think that's it. I'm thinking more that she might've seen something she shouldn't have."

"The fatal shot of insulin?"

"Maybe. Or it might not have had anything to do with Sheila."

"I have a list of everyone on duty in the ER that evening. If I read off the names, can you moan or something when I say her name?"

Solving Sheila's murder was my priority. "Yeah, I can manage that."

Tucker started rattling off the names, and I coughed when he said Christie Singer. "Now that wasn't so hard was it?"

"Do I get a special award for coughing?" I said, picturing Tucker's masculine body.

He chuckled. "That can be arranged."

"Did you find out anything about Vicky Marsh's

death?"

"Her family is part of a class action suit against a climbing gear manufacturer, claiming the gear was faulty. Due to the lawsuit, they have copies of Marsh's hospital records that show she died as a result of a climbing accident. Those records have been scrutinized by the law firm representing the plaintiffs. Victoria Marsh's body was cremated."

"So if, like Sheila, her blood tests were switched, it's too late to do anything about it. And with the lawsuit, her family would be against anyone even questioning her cause of death."

"Exactly. And we have no evidence that indicates she didn't die as a result of a climbing accident. Stan is flagging me down. See you later." Tucker disconnected.

Staring at my cell phone, my mind flashed to an entry in Georgina's journal—"Too much insulin will *also* take care of that problem." An entry she made regarding her husband and before Sheila's death. When Maddie mentioned that Vicky Marsh might've had an affair with Jared, I had thought the "also" could've been referring to Vicky. Even if it was, it would never be discovered.

Feeling disappointed, I grabbed a soda out of fridge and went to the den. I put the listening device on the desk and checked if the bug at April's house had picked up anything. The sound of a door opening and closing a few was all that had been recorded. Since that was the only noise, I surmised the bug was in a closet. Leaving that bug on record, I clicked to the one in Jared's car, a bug I hadn't checked on for several days. No sounds came through the speaker. In case he decided to call someone after his interview with Stan and Tucker, I left it on as I summarized the meeting with Christie and what Tucker told me about his interview with Malcolm and his visit with Bo.

Who has the third weapon? Since Georgina's husband was still alive, it was probably logical that she would have the pistol. Shooting him in the yard and then claiming she thought he was a burglar—something like that. Where would she have hidden it? I searched her bedroom, but didn't look in all the shoeboxes in the closet or under the mattress. Assuming it was in her possession, the gun could've been tucked away some other place in her house, or garage, or trunk of her car.

As I contemplated the possibilities, a clinking noise came from the listening device, followed by a car door opening and snapping shut. Next, I expected to hear the sound of the Porsche engine. Instead I heard tapping.

"Hey," Colleen's voice blared through the speaker, and then I turned down the volume.

"Have you got any plans for tonight?" Jared asked.

"Yes," she said hesitantly. "Georgina and I are going to be questioned about the cabin...tomorrow. Georgina thought we should meet so April can fill us in on the questions the police asked her."

"You've already talked to April about that."

"I know, but she didn't talk to Georgina. I think Georgina is feeling a little left out, so we're going to meet. Oh, how did your questioning go?"

"Not too bad. I told them everything I remembered. Poor Mark. If only..."

"Jared, with two bullets in his chest, no one could've saved him."

"We need to talk."

"Why?" Colleen's voice trembled. Was she worried that he might ask for a divorce or separation? She had followed Georgina each time Georgina meet Jared during the prior week. She knew they were involved.

"I want to tell you about my interview with the detectives before you meet with them tomorrow."

"That's it?" Relief was evident in her tone.

"Yes," Jared said slowly. "What time are you planning to meet with April and Georgina, and where?"

"Eight at Georgina's house."

"Are you home now?"

"Yes."

"I'll be there soon."

When the roar of his engine started, I leaned back in my chair and wondered if Jared had listened to the disk I left him and wanted a long talk with Colleen, more than just discussing his interview. I tapped on the edge of my desk. I knew Colleen had played no part in Mark Holbrook's death, but Sheila's death could be a different matter.

Speculating about the crime wasn't going to get it solved. April would be gone tonight. Besides retrieving my bug, I doubted I'd find anything there that would shed more light on Sheila's case, but I might run across something that could help in Mark's case.

I picked up the phone and called Grover, my boss.

"How's the investigation going?"

"Moving along." My cell beeped, indicating a call was coming in. Ignoring it, I said, Hey, can I use some of your interference equipment tonight?"

"Are you planning to break into a place with sophisticated surveillance equipment?"

"I'm not sure how sophisticated, but there are outside cameras."

"Come by the office. I've got just the right thing for you to use. It's smaller than the one you used last time. I'll only be here for another thirty minutes."

"See you in a few." I disconnected and checked the missed call. It came from Tucker. He had also left me a voice mail saying he'd be home in a couple of hours to tell me about the interview. I checked the time—5:05 p.m.

Chapter 19

It was almost 7:00 p.m. when I returned from Grover's office with the equipment I needed to disarm April's security system, and then some. A problem popped into my head—April's son. *Will he go with her to Georgina's? Or will a babysitter be at her house?*

As I started to make spaghetti, Tucker walked through the door. "Thought I'd be home earlier, but too many problems arose."

"Anything to do with the Sheila case or the Mark case?"

"No. Another homicide."

"So how did Jared's interview go?" I asked while I added the sauce to the cooked sausage.

"Best one so far. He started out with the same scenario as April and Malcolm until Mark Holbrook set up the cans to do some target shooting. Everyone told him that wasn't allowed, but he ignored them. While Mark was shooting, Jared noticed Georgina examining the rifle and then leaning it against the bushes. That was about the same time that Mark wanted April to shoot at the cans. Jared saw Mark forcing his estranged wife to take the gun, but he was too far away to see if she took it before it went off."

"Did he say if Colleen was standing by him?"

"Yes, they were both next to the porch."

"So she probably couldn't have seen any more than he did. And the second shot?"

"Jared was hurrying toward Mark when that shot was fired. He never saw Georgina pick up the rifle, but he *did* notice Malcolm dodging away from his wife."

"So according to Jared, Georgina examined the rifle before it mysteriously appeared in her hand."

Tucker nodded. "Then Jared went into detail, using medical terms, about how he tried to stabilize Mark to no avail. He also took care of the flesh wound Malcolm sustained from the bullet fired from the rifle before it struck Mark. Jared confessed that he'd made an error in judgment not reporting the bullet wounds and for his unethical conduct in helping to bury Mark."

"What will happen to Jared Ebert now?"

"The fact that he didn't report the gunshot wounds will cause him some problems." Tucker grabbed a piece of garlic bread and took a bite. "Jared will probably just end up with a slap on the wrist. The medical board might take some disciplinary action against him, but even without Feister's help, I doubt his medical license is in jeopardy. Jared Ebert is a renowned heart surgeon. His patients come from all over the country." Tucker nodded. "He'll make a good witness."

As he grabbed a couple of beers from the fridge, I set the kitchen table.

"We're not eating in the dining room."

"Nope. I need to take off soon." I dished up the spaghetti.

He picked up his fork. "Doing another illegal break-in?"

"Yep."

"Are you looking for the missing gun?"

"That," I said, between bites and then decided to tell him about the bug, "and the bug I left in Feister's office."

"You didn't snag it when you searched through Georgina's desk?"

"Someone else snagged it before I could."

His brow creased. "Who?"

"Not sure. Yesterday it was at Colleen's house. Today it's at April's. Want to be my lookout?" And then I told him about the gated community and how I knew she wouldn't be home.

"Didn't think the bug you planted in Jared's car would be that useful."

"Neither did I."

April wouldn't be there, so I doubted I'd be in any danger. Still, it might be good having a friendly cop close by if someone spotted me breaking in or out of her house.

Tucker couldn't be seen as aiding and abetting a burglar, which is how it would look if I were caught and we drove to and from the crime scene together. We agreed to each drive our own car.

* * *

I parked on the road abutting the gated community, and Tucker parked about a hundred feet from me. Before venturing to April's house, I checked to make sure the bug was still there. It was. And I hoped her son wasn't. Then I slipped on my auburn wig and hid my eyes under oversized glasses. After throwing my backpack over my shoulder, I took my listening device to Tucker. Once I located the bug, I intended to relay my findings to him, assuming there would be some findings, and I also had it on record so I could document my visit to April's house.

Reaching her house, I saw light peeking through the area around her plantation shutters. I went to her front door and rang the doorbell and waited. Fifteen seconds later, I rang it again. No answer. I leaned closer to the door, listened, and didn't detect any movement inside. In case a neighbor had noticed me, I walked to the end of her cul-de-sac and ducked behind the nearest bush and removed the wig and glasses. Then I stealthily made my way back to April's house.

When I was close to the corner of her house, I slipped on a pair of latex gloves and pulled the signal jammer that Grover had given me out of my pocket and pushed the on button. It jammed cell phone signals, Wi-Fi, and other frequencies within a hundred feet. As soon as I passed her surveillance equipment, I planned to push it off before the neighbors started searching for the cause of the problem.

I clamored over the fence, rushed to the back door, and quickly took care of the lock. The alarm system box was in a hallway a few feet from the door. After disabling it, I took my bug detector out of my backpack, turned it on, and swiftly moved through

her house. It started flashing when I reached the
master bedroom. I closed the door to the hallway and
looked around for small surveillance cameras, though
it was unlikely there would be any in a bedroom.
Satisfied, I turned off the signal jammer and
continued moving the bug detector around. It flashed
more rapidly near the closet. I slid open the door and
the detector led me to a large shoebox. Inside it was a
pair of boots. Running my fingers around them, I
touched my bug and lifted it out. I held it next to my
mouth and said, "Found the bug. Starting my search
of her bedroom." I dropped it in my pocket.

There were only a few shoeboxes in her closet.
Most of her shoes were nicely lined up on three shoe
shelves. Another shoebox, the same size as the one
that had held my bug, sat on a bottom shelf. It had a
hand-drawn star on the side. Wondering if the star
meant anything, I pulled out the shoebox, brushed off
a layer of dust, and looked inside.

My eyes popped wide open when I saw pictures of
Colleen, scantily clothed, lying on a bed in the arms of
a man, not Jared. I placed the box on the floor and sat
down next to it, and thumbed through the pictures. I
stopped when I reached pictures with only Colleen in
them. She was lying on a bed by herself and appeared
to be in the same pose as the first picture. I held up
both pictures. Her pose was a perfect match to the
picture with the guy in it. The couple picture had
been photoshopped. *Why?* I pulled out more pictures
that only featured Colleen. Under those photos were
pictures of the man with different women. Upon
closer examination, the woman had been removed
and Colleen inserted in her place. Did Colleen put
them together to make Jared jealous? Or was April

behind it to tear Colleen and Jared apart? I tended to lean toward the latter, but why would she ruin her sister's marriage? What would April gain? And when Tucker had questioned her, April had protected Colleen, blurting out that Georgina had been in the ER the evening Sheila was brought in. That still struck me as odd. But if Colleen was responsible for the pictures, why store them at her sister's house? From the dust on the box, it had been there for a while, so whoever was responsible for the photoshopped pictures, why not toss them out? I flipped through those at the bottom of the box again and realized there were some pictures with the guy and another woman that weren't among those photoshopped with Colleen inserted in the woman's place. Maybe that was it—at some future time, Colleen's photo could be photoshopped into those pictures, replacing the woman. But why?

Lingering in April's house, speculating about it, wasn't a good idea if I wanted to get my search done. Yet, I continued staring at the photos. Could they have any bearing on the case? I doubted it, but they did show that either April or Colleen knew how to deceive. On that thought, I took out my cell phone and snapped a picture of one of the photoshopped images. No flash. I checked the picture on my cell. It was so dark I couldn't make out the people in it. I attempted to take another picture. Again, no flash. I picked up the box and sat it on top of April's nightstand. After spreading out some photos on her bed, I took a picture and then checked it to make sure it came through clearly. Satisfied, I snapped pictures of several of the photoshopped pictures along with the source photos. To keep Tucker from being bored,

I attached them to a text that read, "Someone is good at photoshopping."

If Tucker hadn't called to tell me that April was at the gate by the time I finished searching for the gun, I'd intended to take photos of the remaining pictures. Leaving the box of pictures in her bedroom, I went back into the closet and looked through the other shoeboxes. No gun. Next, I rummaged through her dresser. Nothing unusual was in any of the drawers. Then recalling April had hidden the cocaine under Georgina's dresser, I pulled out the bottom drawer and smiled. A pistol was on the carpet. Holding it in my gloved hand, I examined it. The serial number had been filed off. "The pistol is under her dresser," I said, relaying the information to Tucker through the bug while I slid the drawer back in place.

Then I went to check her bathroom. On the countertop was a cardboard box filled with prescription bottles. Her name wasn't listed as the patient, but she was the prescribing doctor on all of them. There were a few prescriptions of Ativan, two of Oxycodone, and five of Simvastatin. Did she pick up prescriptions for some of her patients? I opened the medicine cabinet. On the top shelf sat two vials of insulin, two insulin pens, and a bottle of aspirin. The two shelves below it had an assortment of bandages, antiseptics, and toothpaste. The top counter drawer contained combs, brushes, and makeup. The second drawer also contained makeup along with a box of latex gloves. The bottom drawer held syringes with needles and a hairdryer. The cabinet under her sink just held miscellaneous cleaning supplies and a garbage container.

As I stepped back into the bedroom, the door flew

open, and April stood in the doorway. I felt irritated that Tucker hadn't warned me she was on her way. Had something happened to him?

She eyed me up and down. "I figured I'd catch you here."

I noticed one of her hands was behind her back. With the third gun tucked under her dresser, I wondered if she was concealing another type of weapon as I cautiously took a step closer to her.

April swung the hidden hand out in front of her. "Stop right there," she snapped and gestured at the dart she held. "I'm good at throwing these. I've won contests. And this one will render you unconscious within a minute."

"A tranquilizing dart?" I said, hoping Tucker was listening.

Her eyes bore into mine. "A little more than that."

Does it hold a fatal dose of insulin? My eyes swept around the room for something I could use to defend myself if she made a movement to fling the dart. Within arm's reach, a brass lamp stood on the top of her dresser.

Then she pulled another dart out of pocket and removed a covering from the tip. Holding a dart in each hand, April said, "I heard an investigator was snooping around, looking into Sheila's death. Who hired you? My father, the great Dr. Raymond Feister?" Her voice dripped with sarcasm. "Georgina doubts it could be him because you came looking for Sheila's medical records, but he'd never hand over medical records, not even to a hired investigator, without going through proper channels. The old man *does* have ethics. But if he suspected that something had occurred at his hospital—his wonderful, magnificent hospital—that could tarnish its reputation, he'd want to be the first to know. Was he aware you planted a bug in his office?"

I shook my head, not wanting my answer to be recorded.

"I spotted it right after he chastised me and before he ordered me out of his office. Did you get an earful?" She clenched her teeth. "Everything is always my fault. You heard how he treats me." Her eyes became moist. "And his little princess, Colleen, can do no wrong."

To me, that statement confirmed April was behind the photoshopped pictures. Were those pictures the cause of the rift between Colleen and her husband?

She went on. "Tell me, what came to his attention that made him want to have Sheila Wilson's death investigated? The tox report? The other blood tests? How did he find out about them?"

Seeing the documents Feister's lawyer had left regarding the inaccurate toxicology report, I knew Feister was aware of that falsified report, but I didn't have a clue how he discovered it.

She waved the dart in her left hand. "Spit it out."

"He didn't tell me that."

"Sheila and I used to be good friends." Her bottom lip quivered. "She thought I was oblivious to her affair with Jared. How could I be? Colleen borrows my car whenever she thinks Jared is messing around." She pressed her lips together and swallowed hard. "But...but it's not really to spy on him. She worries about him. Can you believe that? Worrying about a cheating husband? Colleen even thought Sheila was good for him. She wanted Jared to be happy. On top of everything, she still loves him."

A couple of Grover's highly experienced investigators have told me that it was common for a perp to tell the victim everything before they fired the fatal shot. Even though April wasn't holding a gun, the darts in her hands could easily deliver the same results. She had no intention of letting me walk out of here. Her goal was either for me to leave in a body bag or die on the way to the ambulance, but I sensed something was off. She didn't seem all that sure of herself. Then I caught April staring at the box on her nightstand, and I inched closer to her.

Her eyes sprang to me. "Not another step." She slightly raised a dart in a trembling hand. "I see you found the box. Colleen and Jared married in college. Two love birds. They couldn't keep their hands off of each other." A muscle in her jaw twitched, and she bit her lower lip. "She was Daddy's princess and Jared's angel. Five years ago, after Mark and I had just celebrated our tenth anniversary, he started cheating on me while Jared remained as loyal as could be. Things had to change. Colleen cried on my shoulder after Jared confronted her about the first set of pictures. She denied having an affair, and somehow managed to smooth it over. The second set showed Colleen and her lover in their bedroom. I also left a few pieces of male clothing under their bed. Clever, huh?

"Now Jared's infidelity matches Mark's...*did* match Mark's." Her eyes drooped, and her face lined with sadness and despair. "Mark's no longer with us...Daddy still believes Colleen is perfect." April's bottom lip quivered again, and then she cleared her throat. "That soon will change."

"How?" I asked, wanting her answer to be

recorded.

"Sheila's accurate blood tests will suddenly appear, and everyone will learn that she died from an overdose of insulin—a fatal limit. Jared, my dear sister's husband, was having an affair with Sheila. That's not a secret among her co-workers. Colleen's a nurse. She was seen in the ER, and there's always a supply of insulin there." Her voice quavered "She...she spent some private time with Sheila. You put it together—motive, means, and opportunity." A tear drizzled down her cheek and she brushed it away with the back of her hand.

"Thought...thought it was only fair to give you a rundown before I use self-defense against a burglar."

As she raised an arm, I grabbed the lamp on her dresser, yanking it out of the socket as I leapt toward her, yelling, "Help!"

At that same moment came the cracking sound of her window being smashed. Shards of glass floated through the room.

I swung the lamp, knocking one dart out of her hand. Moving the lamp in the other direction, I felt a sharp poke in my arm before the other dart tumbled to the floor. Pinning her against the wall, I saw her tear-filled eyes and a sad expression on her face.

"We can handle it from here, Miss," Tucker said, clutching April's hands.

"This is my house." April said, sounding jittery, and then gestured toward me. "She's a burglar."

Stepping backwards, I saw two uniformed cops as my body swayed and my knees buckled. Then everything went black.

Chapter 20

Smelling the aroma of roses, I slowly opened my eyes as sunlight streamed through the room and realized I was lying in a hospital bed.

Tucker stroked by cheek. "How are you feeling, sweetheart?"

Since he seldom called me that, I figured something was terribly wrong as the memories of being in April's bedroom streamed through my head. I swallowed hard and said, "Am I dying?"

He smiled, leaned forward, and kissed my cheek. "No, Dee. The doc said he'd release you later this morning. April did manage to push the tip of a dart into your arm, but the drugs in it couldn't do any permanent harm."

"Drugs? No Insulin?"

Tucker nodded. "No insulin. A mixture of cocaine and a knock-out drug. My guess...she intended to pull out the hidden gun after you were out cold and finish you off."

"Assuming that was her scheme, the tox report would show cocaine in my system, making it appear a druggy had broken into her home, and she'd defended herself."

Tucker nodded. "That's probably how she originally planned for it to go down."

"But if she really believed that I had been hired by her father, she'd know he'd question it."

"What could he do without any proof to the contrary?"

"Why didn't you warn me when she drove through the gate?"

"She never drove or walked through the gate. Her car had a flat tire and was at the side of the road a block away."

"How did you get a couple of cops to go with you to her house?"

A mischievous smile flashed on his face. "An unidentified neighbor reported a burglary was in progress, and your screaming helped. That gave us all the probable cause we needed to enter." He tucked a lose strand of hair behind my ear. "Glad you did that."

"The last thing I heard was her saying it was her house and I was a burglar."

He took my hand. "And that's how it appears right now. You broke into her house and she defended herself. We couldn't bring her in. You're the one with the legal problem for what went down last night."

"I never entered her place with the intent to steal anything or harm anyone. The most I could be charged with would be criminal trespass. What about the cocaine?"

"It wasn't discovered until after you arrived at the hospital. I managed to take the dart with us. Stan plans to use the cocaine to get a search warrant for her house. Going after her for possession of cocaine is minor compared to a potential murder charge."

"Good point. Did you hear everything April said to me?"

"What I didn't hear when you were with her, I caught on the recording. She indirectly confessed to killing Sheila, but that confession was obtained through illegal bugging. We have all the facts. Now we need more admissible proof to substantiate them. If we can get an admissible confession out of her, that would speed things up. April didn't want to give us a statement last night about your break-in. For some reason, she wanted her lawyer present. She'll come in sometime late today or tomorrow, depending on when her attorney is available."

The sad look on April's face streamed into my head. "You heard the recording, but you didn't see her as she spoke. She was nervous and teary-eyed. Something about that struck me as being odd. Not the type of behavior I would expect from someone who had been scheming to take out an investigator."

"Maybe she was struggling with her conscience, but she didn't hesitate using a dart. Inexperienced killers do sometimes get emotional before they shoot someone. That doesn't prevent them from committing the crime."

As I thought about sad-looking April, an idea popped into my head. "Did anyone else hear the recording?"

"No."

That was what I had figured. Playing it for anyone

would only provide proof that I bugged her place. And there would be no way Tucker, an officer of the law, could explain how he had acquired the recording without mentioning me. "How soon do I have to report to jail?" I asked since I had never been in that position before.

"You won't be officially charged until we get a statement from April."

"Why? She told you I was a burglar."

"As we waited for the ambulance, April announced she was a doctor and pushed me aside and gave you medical attention. She must have noticed the concerned look on my face because she told me you'd be all right. After you were secured to the gurney, she leaned closer to your face and said something like, 'Please don't tell my father'."

"Interesting," I said, thinking that added fuel to my idea. "When are you going to be talking to Georgina and Colleen?"

"Georgina Levin's interview is scheduled for one and Colleen Ebert at three."

"It's doubtful that either one of them will say that April had a firm grip on the gun before it went off, striking Mark."

"Georgina might see it differently when she's asked about her purchase of the guns that we dug up."

* * *

"It was shortly before 12:30 p.m. when Tucker drove me to my car. "I'll call you after the interviews are over." He wrapped me in his arms and kissed me deeply. "Go home and rest. Don't do any snooping around today."

I softly kissed his lips. "Don't worry. I promise not to do any breaking in today."

"But you might do some snooping around. Is that what you're saying?"

"You still need evidence to put Sheila's murderer behind bars, and I intend to help you get it—but nothing illegal. At least not for today." I gave him a big smile.

Tucker rolled his eyes. "Glad to hear that."

After I drove home, showered, and dressed, I went into the den and listened to last night's recording. Preparing to put my idea into motion, I copied the recording to a few disks and slipped one in a disk sleeve and the other one in a mailer in case Plan A didn't materialize.

With both disks in my backpack, I climbed into my car and headed to April's house. I parked in my usual spot and glanced at my watch—2:48 p.m. *Colleen will be interviewed soon. She can't be hanging out with April.* I footed it to April's place and saw her car wasn't in the driveway. Then I worried that she had gone with Colleen to the precinct to give the impression of the loving sister.

I still marched to her door and rang the bell.

A few seconds later, the door flew open and there stood April. "What are you doing here?" she snapped.

"I want to talk to you."

"About what?"

"Last night. I don't think you want to take a chance of having anyone overhear what I have to say."

Her eyes studied my face. "Come in, but you need to make it quick. My sister is going to stop by on her way home from the police station, and my son will be home at four-thirty." She opened the door wider.

As I entered, she gestured toward to the couch. Once we were both seated, I pulled the sleeve-covered disk out of my backpack. "The unplanned meeting we had last night was recorded."

Biting her bottom lip, April stared at the disk.

"I'm not here to blackmail you. I'm actually here to find out the truth."

Her eyes remained on the disk as she said, "What truth?"

"Before we get into that, let me start by telling you that I'm not working for your father. Maddie Wilson hired me to look into her aunt's death. At that time, I already knew something was off. I saw Sheila swaying as she walked away from the hospital. And from what you said last night, you are responsible for her death."

April chewed her bottom lip, and her hands trembled.

I continued. "But from how upset you appeared, I got the impression that something was off about what you were saying. And you mentioned Georgina didn't think your father had hired me. Were you discussing the planned murder of Sheila with Georgina and was she somehow involved? I want the truth." I demanded.

"Is what we're talking about being recorded?"

I shook my head. "No. Whatever you say will be kept between us."

Her eyes focused on the disk. "Georgina drugged Sheila. She wanted Sheila out of the way. Do you already know about her and Jared?"

"Yes."

"She wants him to herself."

"What about her husband?" I asked, attempting to obtain more information about what went down at the cabin.

"Georgina planned to kill her husband at a cabin my father owns, but the one that died was Mark." Her eyes became moist, and she clutched her shaking hands. "It was an accident, but I don't think the police believe me." April briefly closed her eyes and a few tears drizzled down her cheeks. "I even reported him missing before going to the cabin. I was so worried about him. His parents and his boss told me he had taken a trip, but I felt something was wrong. He used to call me almost every day, and Mark would never take off without talking to Kyle, our son. The police believed he was on a trip. They wouldn't search for him." She sniffled and wiped her eyes with her fingertips. "I was happy when I saw him at the cabin. He'd remembered my birthday. I thought someday we'd get back together." She rose to her feet. "I'll be right back."

Within a minute, she returned, dabbing a tissue over her cheeks and carrying a box of Kleenex.

"Why didn't you tell anyone that Georgina planned to kill her husband?"

April swallowed hard. "I couldn't. She knows about the pictures. I don't know how she found out, but she knows. She was going to tell Colleen if I didn't help her set it up. And Colleen would hate me. Georgina even made me go with her to pick up the guns." April softly blew her nose. "And then if I didn't help her get rid of Sheila, she was going to tell everyone that I had planned on killing Mark because he was cheating on me. She was even going to say I forced her into buying the guns. Georgina…Georgina is good at lying. She'll make up some kind of story and everyone will believe her."

Georgina was blackmailing her? I had thought she was in cahoots with Georgina. And I already knew Georgina was good at lying from the way she had taken credit for Colleen's plea to get Feister to help Jared keep his license. "Georgina couldn't have known that Sheila was going to be struck by a car. How had she planned to get her into the ER?"

Tears welled in April's eyes. "She…she was going to follow Sheila and gave her a knockout drug… Georgina didn't want to do that in the hospital. Then she'd… disguise her voice and call 911…using a burner phone. Sheila would end up in the ER." April wiped her face again.

"Why did you say all that stuff last night when it wasn't true?"

"Well…well…Georgina wanted Colleen to go to jail for killing Sheila," she said as tears flowed down her cheeks. "I…I thought Georgina might be listening."

"Georgina listening?"

"She knew…the bug you left in my father's office was here and thought you might show up to get it. She sent me home to check. I told her I won't kill anyone else, but she held the pictures and Mark's death over my head again. I had to knock you out." She dabbed a tissue over her face. "I'll never be free from her."

"So you thought Georgina was close by to make sure you did it?" After April nodded, I asked, "Then what? Would Georgina appear and finish the job?"

April nodded again. "I was supposed to call her, but I spotted her hiding near my house."

"The darts? Did Georgina give those to you?"

She shook her head. "No. I already had those. I was afraid Georgina might sneak into my house and try to kill me to make sure I never squealed."

Given what she had said about Georgina, I suspected she had good reason to fear her. "Have you talked to her after the police left last night?"

She shook her head.

April might have been right that Georgina was within earshot. Otherwise, I would've anticipated that she'd want to know what went wrong the prior night that caused the police and ambulance to show up at April's house.

"April, you have to go to the police and confess to killing Sheila before Georgina turns on you. Look at the way she turned on Jared in the meeting with your father, and she'll turn on you too to save her hide."

"Her blurting that out about Jared surprised me. She wanted me to hide...ah...something in her house. Left off the alarm so I could do it, and then she acted like I was out to get her just because I didn't have a chance to tell her where I hid it before she found it."

That was another thing I didn't get right. I had also thought April wanted Georgina to be caught with the cocaine.

"You need to tell the police everything about how Georgina was blackmailing you—both about what went down at the cabin and Sheila's death."

"But the pictures...Colleen will hate me."

"Confess to Colleen why you photoshopped those pictures and let her know you couldn't find a way to make it right without her hating you. Then explain how you allowed Georgina to blackmail you because you feared she would destroy your relationship with your sister and father.

"Relationship with my father? He'd probably just as soon have me locked up."

"That's not true. After you were dismissed from his office, he mentioned to Colleen that you were a good doctor and wished you could handle your personal life better. He talked like a caring father, not someone who wanted you out of his life."

"Really?" April said as more tears filled her eyes.

I patted her hand. "Really."

"But they'll both hate me for killing Sheila."

"April, I can't give you any guarantees, but once they know the truth about how it happened, there's a stronger possibility that you can maintain a relationship with them than if they thought you were working with Georgina to try to have Colleen take the fall for killing Sheila. And that's exactly how it might appear if Georgina gets cornered and decides to drag you down with her."

While April wiped away more tears, I glanced at my watch—4:05 p.m. "Keep the disk. Listen to it if it'll help you make a decision. Whatever you decide to do, destroy it."

With a trembling hand, she picked it up and handed it to me. "No. Take it. I don't want it here. Every night since...I keep seeing Sheila's face. Guilt... I'm a doctor...Doctors are supposed to help save lives...not kill no matter what...being blackmailed isn't an excuse." Tears streamed down her face again. "I can't take it anymore. It's good...that my father suspended me from the hospital. Sheila...Sheila was constantly on my mind, and I wasn't giving my all to my patients, like they deserve." She wiped away the tears. "I'm going to confess to Colleen when she gets here. Do you think...she'll go with me to the police station?"

"I don't know, April, but ask her. I've seen the way she treats you. Colleen loves you." I stuck the disk back into my backpack. "I need to get going before Colleen gets here."

April stayed on the couch, sobbing, as I left her house.

Climbing into my car, I saw a dark blue Mercedes, Colleen's car, turn toward April's community gate.

Driving home, I thought about April. She always believed she lived in Colleen's shadow. Her father reinforced that when he always took Colleen to social events after Colleen turned sixteen. Pictures of Feister with his daughter had often appeared in the social section of the newspaper. April was left out. I never knew he had another daughter until I started this investigation. Maybe she became a doctor in hopes that would make her father proud of her. Poor April. It was obvious from everything I heard that her sister deeply loved her. I doubted she'd shun her after learning about the pictures and Sheila's murder, but I wasn't sure how her father would react. Even knowing his daughter had only committed the crime because she was being blackmailed, would he help her or walk away and make her fend for herself?

Chapter 21

Sitting in the reclining chair with my legs up, I felt tired from the prior night's unwelcome dart poke like the doctor told me I would. He had also said that I shouldn't drive a car or operate any heavy equipment for at least twelve hours. It was good that Tucker wasn't in the room when he said that. Had I followed the doctor's medical advice, I wouldn't be anxiously waiting to hear if April had confessed. She said she would, but she could've changed her mind. I doubted that since she knew about the recording, but that possibility did exist.

I stared at the clock on the wall and watched the minutes tick away and had the urge to call Maddie to tell her who murdered her aunt. It was too early to do that. Right now all I had was an illegal recording that contained a woman's confession. It didn't accurately portray why Sheila was killed. Even if it did, it couldn't be used to bring justice for Sheila, and I couldn't even tell Maddie about it. So, I had nothing to report to her.

Finally at 6:40 p.m., my cell rang.

"Hey," Tucker said. "What a day. First Georgina and then Colleen gave the same flow of events leading up to Mark's death as April gave when she was questioned about it. Georgina adamantly claimed she never touched the rifle before it suddenly appeared in her hands and accidentally discharged. Colleen doesn't recall seeing anyone picking up any of the weapons except for Mark.

"Things got a little more interesting when Sheila was brought up. Georgina said she had never met her but had heard that she wasn't well liked. When I asked for more specifics, she told Stan and me all about Sheila's fling with Jared Ebert and how upset Colleen had been about the adulterous affair."

"Georgina called it an 'adulterous affair'?"

"Exact words. She even mentioned seeing Colleen in the hospital that dreadful day. Now let me get to the good part. When I was getting ready to leave, April Holbrook came into the precinct with her sister. Sheila's death had been haunting her, and she couldn't handle it any longer. She confessed, but the motive she gave for killing Sheila, didn't jive with the recording."

"That's because what we heard last night wasn't all true. Only the part about the photoshopped pictures was accurate. I told you something was off, so I paid her a visit today."

"So you already know about Georgina blackmailing her?"

"Yes. April thought Georgina was listening. That's the reason she didn't tell the truth. She couldn't exactly spill the truth with the blackmailer listening. Georgina knew the bug was at April's house. She had sent April home to check if I was there. April hadn't planned on killing me. That job was going to be handled by Georgina after I was knocked out."

"A few neighbors had gathered outside April's house when the ambulance arrived," Tucker said. "Georgina could've easily been among them. Like you, I thought there was a chance that Georgina and April were partners in crime. Must admit, when April gave her statement and talked about being blackmailed, neither Stan nor I had seen that coming. Since April was crying when she showed up at the station, Colleen Ebert sat next to her the whole time. With her sobbing, we often had to stop so she could compose herself. Later, she mentioned that you had not broken into her house and she was sorry for accusing you of burglary. Did you play a hand in convincing her to confess?"

"Possibly, but she kept having nightmares ever since she killed Sheila. I might have speeded up her confession, but she would have eventually done it on her own. Even though, she committed a regrettable crime, April seems like a good person that made terrible mistakes. Do you think her sister and father will stand by her?"

"They're both here hugging and comforting her. Right after she confessed and finished making her statement, Feister showed up with the attorney who'll be representing April. He was irritated with Colleen that she didn't stop April from confessing until an attorney was present. April told her father that Colleen had tried to stop her, but she couldn't hold off any longer."

I felt relieved for April. Her family wouldn't abandon her. "Oh, Mark Holbrook's death really was an accident."

"That had already been determined before April arrived at the precinct."

"So what's next?"

"Based on the evidence we've gathered, April's statement, and her saved text and voice messages, the bullet Georgina fired wasn't by mistake. It just didn't hit the intended target."

"April had saved text and voice messages from Georgina?"

"Yes. She didn't tell you about those?"

"No."

"So I learned something today before you did."

"Do the messages confirm she was being blackmailed?" I asked because I had been worried that it could be a she-said-she-said thing. Georgina could give a whole different slant on what had occurred, and April wouldn't be able to substantiate that Georgina had been blackmailing her.

"Yes. The voice messages have already been authenticated. The text messages are currently being worked on. Even without them, we have enough evidence. Sometime this evening, Georgina will be arrested for the attempted murder of her husband. She'll also be charged in the death of Sheila once we've completed the interviews of more hospital personnel and determined how and where she drugged Sheila."

"Suppose you can't find any witnesses that she drugged Sheila, then what?"

"In a text message, she told April she had done it. Once those messages are substantiated, that might be enough. It depends on the D.A. Jared Ebert just walked in. I'll be home after April is booked."

I sighed. "Maddie is going to be so glad."

"Regardless of your illegal means, you were the one who solved the case, and that calls for a celebration. Champagne tonight."

"Without your help, it wouldn't have happened."

"My part was minor. See you in a few."

The minute I hung up, I called Maddie and grinned from ear to ear as I gave her the news.

She began bawling. "I knew you could find the killer," she sniffled, and then I heard Tobias's muffled voice in the background.

"We're both so grateful to you, Dora," Tobias said over the line as Maddie cried. "Maddie will call you tomorrow. Bye, Dora, and thanks again."

As I walked into the bathroom, wanting to take a hot bath before Tucker came home, tears flowed from my eyes like the dam had just burst. My emotions collided. Part of me was happy and relieved the murderer was behind bars, and at the same time, the loss of Sheila was settling in. She had been like a mother to Maddie, and now all that remained were memories.

Sobbing, I filled the tub and sprinkled in bubble bath while the bathroom steamed up. The extra-warm water soothed me as I wiped my tear-streaked face and climbed in. Leaning back, I inhaled and exhaled deeply and forced myself to get my emotions under control and wipe out the events of the prior two weeks from my mind. I only wanted to think about Tucker. I closed my eyes and envisioned his well-built body and gorgeous smile. Hearing the door squeak open, I sat up straight and saw the man of my dreams walk in, carrying a bottle of champagne and two flutes.

Without saying a word, his eyes glowed as he removed his clothing. Then he gave me that sensuous smile I loved, filled the flutes, and handed me one. "To my gal," he said and clicked my glass with his. He took a sip and slid into the tub behind me.

About the Author

Inge-Lise Goss, a USA Today bestselling and multi-award winning author, was born in Denmark, raised in Utah, and now lives in the foothills of Red Rock Canyon with her husband and their dog, Ted. She spends most of her time in her den writing stories. There, with her muse by her side, her imagination has no boundaries, and her dreams come alive. When she's not pounding away on the keyboard, she can be found reading, rowing, or trying to perfect her golf game, which she fears is a lost cause.

Website: http://www.Inge-LiseGoss.com